She nibbled her berries, watching him

from time to time out of the corner of her eye until their bowls were empty. Then he gave her a long look, and she thought she saw the faint shadow of a smile touch his lips. The heat emanating from his body, the faint odor of dust and sweat and coffee stopped her heartbeat for an instant. She sneaked another glance at him.

His eyes were closed, but he lifted his face to the sky and inhaled, exhaled, inhaled, almost as if waiting for something. And then he opened his eyelids and turned to look at her.

She sucked in her breath at what she saw. He blinked, but not before she saw the moisture that shone in his eyes. Again the ghost of a smile crossed his face. It was gone so quickly she wondered if she had imagined it....

* * *

The Scout
Harlequin Historical #682—November 2003

Acclaim for Lynna Banning

"Do not read Lynna Banning expecting
some trite, cliched Western romance.
This author breathes fresh air into the West."
—*Romance Reviews*

The Angel of Devil's Camp
"This sweet charmer of an Americana romance
has just the right amount of humor, poignancy
and a cast of quirky characters."
—*Romantic Times*

The Courtship
"*The Courtship* is a beautifully written tale
with a heartwarming plot."
—*Romance Reviews Today* (www.romrevtoday.com)

The Law and Miss Hardisson
"…fresh and charming…
a sweet and funny yet poignant story."
—*Romantic Times*

LYNNA BANNING

The Scout

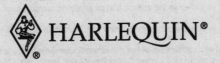

HARLEQUIN®

TORONTO • NEW YORK • LONDON
AMSTERDAM • PARIS • SYDNEY • HAMBURG
STOCKHOLM • ATHENS • TOKYO • MILAN • MADRID
PRAGUE • WARSAW • BUDAPEST • AUCKLAND

ISBN 0-373-29282-1

THE SCOUT

This edition published by arrangement with Harlequin Books S.A.

® and TM are trademarks of the publisher. Trademarks indicated with ® are registered in the United States Patent and Trademark Office, the Canadian Trade Marks Office and in other countries.

Visit us at www.eHarlequin.com

Printed in U.S.A.

Available from Harlequin Historicals and
LYNNA BANNING

Western Rose #310
Wildwood #374
Lost Acres Bride #437
Plum Creek Bride #474
The Law And Miss Hardisson #537
The Courtship #613
The Angel of Devil's Camp #649
The Scout #682

Please address questions and book requests to:
Harlequin Reader Service
U.S.: 3010 Walden Ave., P.O. Box 1325, Buffalo, NY 14269
Canadian: P.O. Box 609, Fort Erie, Ont. L2A 5X3

For my brother, Andrew Yarnes.

With grateful thanks to Suzanne Barrett,
David Woolston, Susan Renison, Tricia Adams,
Bonnie Hamre, Joan Powell, Brenda Preston,
Norma Pulle and Carol Vaughn.

Prologue

Nebraska Territory, 1860

Eleven white-sailed schooners crawled over the heat-shimmered plain, the oxen plodding forward to the snap of a bullwhip. The lead wagon, guided by a large-bellied man with an unbuttoned vest over his loose-sleeved shirt, veered north. The next wagon followed, a short dumpling of a woman in a yellow poke bonnet perched on the driver's bench. Her long-limbed husband walked alongside, prodding the oxen with a goad stick.

Gradually the line turned in on itself until it formed a lumpy circle. The seventh wagon, the largest, painted bright blue with a crisp white canvas cover, lurched forward as the driver jockeyed into position. The young woman on the bench flapped the reins and talked to herself. Her dark hair straggled from beneath a wide-brimmed man's hat, and the sleeves of her brown dress were rolled above her elbows.

At the top of the hill to the west, a single Cheyenne brave, one arm twisted at an odd angle, crouched among the granite and jasper rocks counting the horses.

Chapter One

I write this by moonlight, as it is so bright I need no candle. Sister sleeps inside the wagon, which is stifling hot, but she refuses to join me underneath where it is somewhat cooler, as she still professes her fear of snakes. It is too dusty for snakes, I tell her, but she will not be moved. I cannot blame her. It seems only yesterday we had a roof over our heads, and now we are a month out of Independence sleeping under an open sky.

I am worn to a nubbin. The heat is suffocating and the wind never stops blowing. The fine, silty dirt blows in our faces, into our hair, into our shoes. My teeth are gritty with it! Tonight even the crickets have been baked into silence. My hands are so dry and cracked Mama would turn over in her grave if I touched the tea service.

*A hundred times each day I wonder if I have made
the right decision.*

"Cissy, come quick!"

Constance sat up so fast her forehead banged into
the axle. She rubbed the spot until the ache began
to subside. "What is it?"

"Hurry!" her sister's voice commanded from the
dark interior of the wagon.

She shoved her stockinged feet into the trail-worn
leather boots she kept under her pillow and crawled
out into the open. One big step onto the wagon
tongue, another on the driver's bench, and then she
dove through the gathered bonnet and into the
wagon.

"What's the matter?" She kept her voice low. No
use waking the sleepers in the other wagons just for
one of Nettie's fancies.

"I thought I heard something," her sister whispered. "There...there it is again, a scratching
sound."

"Probably a field mouse. Or maybe it's Mr. Nyland in the next wagon. You know he snores something fierce."

"Cissy, I'm scared."

Constance groped her way past their mother's
carved oak sideboard and knelt on the pallet beside

her sister. "We're all scared, Nettie. If we weren't, we'd be locked up in an asylum." She laid her palm against her sister's damp cheek.

Nettie clutched at her hand. "I wake up in the night and I hear things, noises. Sometimes I'm so frightened I can scarcely breathe."

"It's probably just the horses. Or maybe a coyote."

"I wish I were hearing carriage wheels or a church bell or Mrs. Cortland playing the piano after supper. I can't help it, Cissy, I do."

Constance let out a soft breath. "I know. I wouldn't mind hearing a church bell myself. I get awfully tired of wagon wheels scrunching across miles and miles of tickle grass. It sounds just like Mr. Nyland, only it lasts all day long!"

A hiccup of laughter told her Nettie's spirits were reviving. "Mr. Duquette says we're almost to Fort Kearny." She forced a lightness into her tone. "We've come over three hundred miles since April first."

Nettie sniffled. "I wish we'd never left Ohio."

Constance pressed her fingers against her mouth. Nettie was seventeen, no longer a child. But ever since Papa died, she had wept over every little thing. If only she would *try*.

"Just think, Nettie. One day we'll tell our children about this journey, how we came out west in a spanking new wagon Papa bought with the bank money. We'll tell them all about the water holes and the grasshoppers and how the dust collects under our shimmies and what we ate and…''

Nettie rolled away from her.

Constance cocked her head, listening to the rhythm of her sister's breathing. She would not let herself cry until Nettie was asleep.

By the time the sky turned from black to pale peach, Constance had paced four times around the knot of wagons, dried her eyes with the hem of her skirt and crawled back onto her pallet.

''Mr. Duquette! Mr. Duquette!''

Booted feet thumped past the wagon at a dead run. Constance rolled onto her side and watched another pair of legs trudge by in the same direction. Then she heard Joshua Duquette's raspy before-breakfast voice.

''Now hold on a minute. What are you two Norskies complainin' about?''

''T'ree of my horses are missing,'' a male voice shouted. ''I tell you ve should haf kept them inside the wagon circle.''

That would be Arvo Ollesen. In addition to their riding mounts, Arvo and his brother Cal were herding a dozen mares along the trail west, nurse-maiding them as if they were wives and not just livestock. Constance didn't really blame them; she felt the same about Molly, their cow. Molly was all the family she and Nettie had left.

Cal's accusing voice broke into Mr. Duquette's low rumble. "Vat ve gonna do in Oregon without our mares, eh, mister? Cannot breed horses only with males."

"Stop yer bellyachin'. You got ten good animals left."

"Nine. Ve got nine left. And ve bellyache until you be more careful with our ownings."

Three pairs of boots stomped past the wagon in the opposite direction. Constance waited until the voices faded before she slipped out of bed and clambered up into the interior to dress. Then she would walk down to the stream and bring back a bucket of water for Nettie to wash in.

The soft predawn air smelled of grass. She opened her mouth and sucked in a huge breath, so clean and pungent it made her giddy. She'd never smelled anything like it. Each night she fell into bed so exhausted she could barely move; each morning the sweet-smelling breeze and the cloudless blue sky above her lifted her spirits and set her on her feet again.

She made her way past the Ollesen's makeshift corral, double rope lengths strung between their weathered gray wagon and two cottonwood trees, and all at once a guttural shout stopped her in her tracks.

"Hold it right there, girl."

Constance winced. The wagon train leader. The man was as bossy as any governess she'd ever had.

"Good morning, Mr. Duquette. Mr. Ollesen."

"Just where d'ya think y'er traipsin' off to so early?"

"Down to the stream to fetch water." She kept her tone even, but it was an effort.

"Not this mornin', missy," the large man snapped. "Got Indians hereabouts. Stole a couple of horses last night."

"T'ree horses," Arvo corrected. His square, earnest face looked beyond her to his brother. Cal was his twin except in age and height. Neither man looked sturdy enough to survive in a high wind, but both were strong. Cal and Arvo hitched up her oxen every morning and unhitched them each evening in exchange for clean shirts and underdrawers on wash day.

"I am sure the Indians have gone. My sister and I need some using-water, so if you will ex—"

"I said no!" Duquette shouted. "Indians sneak

around real quiet.'' He angled his long arm in the direction of the stream. ''Nobody's safe out there.

''And another thing,'' he continued. ''Your wagon's bigger'n all the others. When we pull out this morning, you take the tail position.''

Constance blinked in surprise. ''But…but yesterday we were seventh in line. Should we not be eighth instead of last?''

Duquette spat off to one side. ''Told you when we started we'd have no arguments. I'm the wagon master, elected fair and square, so you'll do as I say.''

Worse than a governess. Joshua Duquette was a dictator of the first water. A month on the trail with him had been like marching with a Prussian general.

She pressed her lips together and turned away. Well, *she* hadn't voted for him. She had favored sensible, soft-spoken Abraham Nyland, even if he did snore.

Chapter Two

Colonel Harrison Butterworth looked up when the plank door of his office scraped open. "Major Montgomery," the adjutant announced.

The colonel rose as the tall, lean figure appeared in the doorway. Leaner now, he noted. No wonder in that. The wonder was that he was standing up at all.

He answered the major's salute, then stepped around his desk and extended his hand. "Welcome back to Fort Kearny, John. It's good to see you looking so...it's good to see you."

A flicker of something crossed Montgomery's tanned face. Humor? Distaste? Either one would be a good sign, the colonel decided.

"Take a chair." He gestured toward the straight-backed chair in the corner.

"I'll stand."

"Stand at ease, then. Cricks my neck looking up at you."

The tall man didn't move a muscle.

"Smoke if you want."

"Thanks." But he made no move toward the pocket in his tan buckskin shirt. Instead, he slid one foot apart from the other and relaxed his stance. His boots weren't polished, the general noted. Maybe it was still too soon.

The two men regarded each other in silence for a full minute. The major's ordinarily sharp blue eyes looked flat, like rain-dampened granite. A chill went up the colonel's spine at the change. At least the man no longer walked with a limp. What remained was a wound that burned gut deep.

"Major—"

"The answer is no."

"Well hell, I haven't even asked you yet! Let a man finish."

"Answer's still no."

The older man drew in a long breath. "I could make it an order."

Major Montgomery's gaze shifted to the single window behind the colonel's desk. "You could."

Butterworth sighed. "It's been six months. Almost seven. Your hide still that raw?"

"Nope. Just stubborn. Maybe a little scared."

The general barked a laugh. "Now that's a first. Never known you to be scared."

"Any damn fool in this man's army is scared. Either that or he's lying."

"Just never heard you admit it before," the colonel said in a gentle tone.

"Never been scared before."

Colonel Butterworth's shaggy gray eyebrows arched. "Major, I won't mince words. My scouts report a small wagon train heading our way. They want an escort for the next few hundred miles through Indian country."

"Escort! You and I both know Indians haven't attacked a wagon train in over a year."

"Yeah, well it seems they lost a couple of horses night before last, and their leader, one Joshua Duquette, imagines the sky is falling. Thinks they'll all be massacred."

"Damn fool," the major breathed. "He thinks one horse-soldier ridin' at his side will let him sleep nights? Let him learn the hard way."

"It'll just be hand-holding, Major. No action. That's what—"

The major's low voice bit out two words. "Why me?"

"For one thing, right now I can spare you. And

for another, it'll give you something to do while you…decide on your future.''

''No.''

The colonel's voice dropped. ''I'm making it an order, John. Take Billy West with you.''

Major Montgomery groaned. ''That an order, too?''

In spite of himself, Colonel Butterworth laughed. ''You ever try to give that wily old fox an order?'' He strode forward and clasped the younger man's hand.

''Good luck, Major. You know I wouldn't ask this if I didn't think—'' He coughed and started over. ''I need to provide an escort. And you need to…well, you need to get moving. Otherwise you're going to rot inside.''

Major Montgomery extricated his hand and snapped a salute. ''Mind your own business, Harry.''

''When hell freezes over, John.'' The older man grinned. ''Dismissed.''

Constance climbed up on the driver's bench and spied a long-faced Cal Ollesen striding toward her, a rifle balanced on his bony shoulder.

'''Scuse, please, Miss Constance. Mr. Duquette

said I vas ride in your wagon today, keep lookout for Indians.''

Constance sighed. "Any Indian with half a brain and a stolen horse will be riding away from us, not trailing us."

"Mr. Duquette don't t'ink so."

"Mr. Duquette is a jittery old—" she hesitated a split second "—maid."

Cal turned earnest blue eyes on her. "Dot is reason he put you last in line today. Your vagon bigger than the others, so I can ride inside to keep watch. Please, Miss Constance. I got to do vat he say."

Constance sighed. He was only a boy, trying to follow orders. At her nod, Cal clunked the gun onto the bench and climbed up beside her.

"Don't say anything to Nettie about Indians, will you? She's feeling a bit…skittish this morning."

"Yah, like my mare, Ilsa, I bet. She is feeling same way."

She shot him a look. "No, not like your mare, Cal. Nettie has lost her father and has left behind everything she has ever known. It is hard on her."

"You, too, leave everyt'ing behind."

Constance looked to the grass-covered plains beyond the cottonwood grove. "I am older."

And stronger, she added silently. She'd watched over Nettie for the past eleven years, been both mother and sister to her. After Mama died, Constance had resolved that nothing—*nothing!*—was going to hurt Nettie ever again.

Cal ran two fingers through his mop of curly blond hair. "Iss all right, Miss Constance?"

"Go on back in the wagon, Cal. "You can use the extra bed pillow for a cushion."

She lifted the reins and peered ahead to where Nettie walked off to the left, surrounded by a knot of children. Two of them, Essie and Ruth Ramsey, were so small their short legs took two steps to every one of Nettie's. She held their hands, one on each side, and the boys, Parker, Elijah and Jamie, followed. All Ramseys. Mrs. Ramsey rode in their wagon with a new baby girl.

Nettie's clear voice floated back to her. "A story? Well, now, what kind of story? One about a dragon? Or about…two little girls? Or, let me think…" She twisted to check on the stair-step-sized boys in her wake. "What about a boy named Elijah?"

Constance smiled. Her sister's assigned task was to prevent the younger children from falling beneath the wagon wheels. To keep them in check, she told stories and made up games along the way. She also taught them their sums and letters as they walked, but that was her own idea. Nettie was a born teacher.

"The children—" Nettie had confessed, "Ruth

and Essie and the boys, they take my mind off…
things.''

Constance wondered if Mrs. Ramsey knew what
a blessing her offspring were for her sister. During
the day, she lapped up the adoration of the Ramsey
brood like a hungry cat. Nettie loved being the center of attention. Ever since Mama died, Nettie could
not be loved enough.

Only at night in the privacy of their wagon did
she confess her fears and complain about how tired
she was.

A shout came from the head of the train. Constance snapped her whip, and the oxen strained forward. The iron-covered wagon wheels began to turn.

''You recall that time we was camped by the Big
Blue, John?'' Billy West patted his mare's neck and
chuckled. ''You was just a lieutenant, with soapsuds
behind yer ears, and this gaggle of Sioux braves rode
by just as we stripped for a rinse in the river.''

John grunted. He remembered all right. Seemed
like a good idea at the time, a bath after eighteen
days on the trail. He was so parched he couldn't
decide which to do first—drink or dive in headfirst.

''’Member how those braves lined up along the
bank, laughin' at us?''

John grunted again. "They were laughing at you, Billy. Indians don't wear long red underdrawers."

"Oh, no they wasn't. It was you they got their tongues tangled up over, when you walked outta the water with yer pecker standin' straight up."

John said nothing.

"Most peckers kinda shrink up in water that cold."

"I wasn't thinking about it. I was going for my rifle, trying to save your scrawny neck."

Billy West shook with silent laughter. "Hell you was. You was thinkin' 'bout your woman, plain as day. Well, now, that's perfectly natural, except in the middle of a river with seven braves pointin' fingers at you. Funny how a woman does that to a man, distracts him, I mean. I never will forget the look on your—"

The major shifted in the saddle. "Best keep your mind on the trail, Billy. Wagons shouldn't be too far ahead." He pushed the wide-brimmed hat off his forehead, studied the rolling grassland ahead.

"How come we're trailin' them, instead of meetin' them head-on? Seems like a lotta extra trouble, circlin' around behind."

John let out a slow breath. "Wagon master's green. Maybe trigger-happy. Don't want to give him a target, in case he's nearsighted, too."

Billy nodded. "I knowed that," he muttered under his breath. "Just checkin'." He sent a quick look to the man at his side. "Don't do nuthin' without some good reason, do you, Major?"

The major's steady blue eyes met his. "Not anymore."

Billy looked off into the distance. "Yeah, well, I knowed that, too. Sure am sorry, John."

They rode in silence for a good half hour before Billy couldn't stand it another minute. "You recall that other time, after you was made captain, when the sky opened up and snowed on us in July? One minute it's all blue heaven and me sweatin' so hard I'm like to drown, and the next we're lost in a ground blizzard. I thought we was both dead men."

John remembered that event as well. Remembered fighting through snowdrifts higher than a man could reach, struggling for every foothold. They lost one horse, clung to the other until morning came and the sun rose.

He shook off the memory. Feeling the way he did now, it might have been better if he'd died then and gotten it over with.

"An' then there was the time—"

"Billy, for God's sake, shut up."

"There they are!" the older man shouted. He

shaded his eyes with a battered felt hat. "Them wagons sure move slow."

The two men spurred their horses at the same instant, riding hard until they drew within fifty yards of the last wagon, a blue-painted schooner with red wheels. Suddenly a flash of fire spit from the canvas curtain and a bullet zinged past them.

Constance bolted upright at the sound of the gunshot. "Cal," she shouted. Oh Lord, Indians. Mr. Duquette was right.

Without slowing, the two men following the train separated and zigzagged their mounts until they caught up to the wagon, one on each side.

Hoofbeats pounded close. "Nettie," Constance screamed. "Run. *Run!*"

A dark horse swerved toward her from the left. A man in dark blue trousers and a butter-colored shirt grabbed the wagon frame and levered his body onto the bench beside her. Instinctively she raised her whip hand.

He caught her wrist. "Pull this damn thing up," he yelled. In the next moment he vanished into the interior.

Constance hauled on the traces with all her strength. A scuffling sound came from the back of the wagon, then a yelp.

"Cal? Cal, are you all right?"

No answer. "Cal?"

"He's all right, ma'am," a low voice said. "Just working up an apology."

Some mumbled words, and then Cal poked his head through the bonnet. "Sorry, Miss Constance. I f-fire before I see clear."

Using both hands, Constance set the brake, then leaned back to let her pounding heart slow to normal. Cal climbed out and settled beside her. She could feel his thin frame shuddering.

"A fine pair we are," she managed. "We're both shaking like wet chickens." She attempted a smile.

A giggle escaped the boy's white lips. "Yah, chickens. Who iss that man, d'ya spose? He t'row Mr. Duquette's rifle out of the vagon."

The same low voice now spoke at her elbow. "Name's John Montgomery." The man's gaze slid past her to Cal. "Didn't anyone ever tell you to look before you shoot?"

Cal gulped. "I thought you vas an Indian."

"Take another look," the man snapped.

Nettie ran toward the wagon, a child's hand clutched in hers. "Cissy, what happened?"

"Nothing, pet. Just a—" she flicked a glance at the tall man beside her "—misunderstanding."

A second man with a drooping salt-and-pepper mustache trotted up on a piebald mare. He led the dark horse behind him, and laid the reins in the tall man's palm.

"Thanks, Billy." The man turned away to mount just as Nettie came to a stop in front of him. He stepped out of her path. "Ma'am."

"It's 'Miss'," Nettie replied with a gay smile. "I am…not married."

The tall man nodded once. "Miss."

"Henrietta Weldon," Nettie volunteered, her voice silky. "Lately of Logan County, Ohio."

Constance gaped at her. Until this moment, Nettie hadn't spoken so much as a "Good morning" or "Good evening" to any man on the train, even young Cal Ollesen, who gazed at her with sheep's eyes when she wasn't looking.

The older man chuckled. "My name's Billy West, in case y'er interested. Sure looks like you've got a passel of young-uns." He waved his hand at the Ramsey children hugging Nettie's skirt.

Nettie's gaze remained on Mr. Montgomery's face. "I am very pleased to meet you." There was a lilt in her voice Constance had not heard since they had left home.

Joshua Duquette thrust his flushed face into the circle. "What in tarnation's goin' on back here? You ladies holdin' a social?"

"Are you Duquette?" the tall man inquired.

"Yeah. Just who the hell are you?"

Billy West coughed. "That's Major John D. Montgomery. You might not've heard of him, but he's the man who—"

"Shut up, Billy."

"Sure, Major. I just thought—"

"Colonel Butterworth sent us out from Fort Kearny to escort your wagon train."

"Oh, well, in that case—" Duquette thrust out a sweaty hand "—you're just in time."

Chapter Three

John surveyed the man who planted his bulky frame in front of him. "Just in time for what?" Still holding the wagon master's gaze, he spoke to his friend. "Billy, find the kid's rifle. I tossed it out the back of the wagon."

Duquette's eyes widened. "You threw my rifle— now look here, mister..."

"Major," Billy West reminded. At John's look, he nosed his horse away and headed back down the trail.

Duquette's breathing sounded wheezy and irregular. "That's downright peculiar behavior in my book," he announced. "You come ridin' up behind us, creepin' up like Indians and scaring the ladies half to death. I don't blame Cal here one bit for firing on you."

"Didn't you tell him there'd be an escort?"

The wagon master ignored the question. "How'd he know you were military? Neither one of you's dressed in any kind of uniform. Hell, mister, uh, Major, you're wearin' a damn buckskin shirt!" He jabbed his forefinger against John's chest. "Looks just like an Injun war shirt with all that fringe on it."

He drew his finger back to poke him again, but John brushed his hand to one side. "You finished?"

Duquette opened his mouth, then closed it with a click.

"Then listen up. Out here on the plains, the army doesn't dress to regulation, but the insignia on my hat's plain enough. Not many Indians embroider crossed sabers on their war bonnets."

Duquette looked away.

John glanced at the wiry young man beside him. "If you want to live to see Oregon, you won't shoot at something unless you need it for food. And whether it's a white man or an Indian, you'll hold your fire until there's good cause. Understood?"

Cal bobbed his head.

The wagon master made a growling noise in his throat. "We got good cause."

John swallowed the bitter taste in his mouth. "Think about this, Duquette. If you shoot me, you'll have a small party of cavalry riding after you. You shoot an Indian in these parts, you'll have a whole band of Sioux or Cheyenne warriors on your neck.''

Duquette spat off to one side. ''You know so much, Major, just what're we supposed to do to keep 'em from stealing our horses?''

''Picket them so close you can smell them and set a watch at night.''

He reached for the rifle Billy had retrieved, removed the firing cap and handed the gun to the wagon master. ''Any more questions?

''I haf got a question, mister.'' Arvo Ollesen stepped forward from the clot of gathered onlookers and jerked his head toward Billy's sleek piebald mare in the distance. ''Where'd Mr. West get that spotted horse?''

''It was a gift,'' John said shortly. ''Duquette, you care to parley?''

The two men walked off a short distance from the wagons and faced each other. Constance watched the major spread his long legs and hook both thumbs in his belt. Duquette was doing all the talking, but he avoided looking at Major Montgomery.

Nettie stepped in close to the wagon. ''What is he saying, Cissy?''

Constance looked down into her sister's perfect heart-shaped face, recognized the purposely guileless expression in her eyes. "I don't know. It's not polite to eavesdrop, Nettie."

Nettie shrugged. "Come on, children. Let's gather some buttercups for your mother, shall we?"

Constance glanced at the two men. The major stood motionless while the wagon leader gestured with one thick hand.

The children fanned out, pouncing on the button-shaped yellow blooms and cramming their fists full as Nettie moved among them, pointing out new patches, bending to admire their bouquets. She sidled closer and closer to Duquette and the tall major, and suddenly Constance guessed her intent.

"Nettie?" She waved to catch her sister's eye. Nettie merely smiled and turned her back.

Constance looped the reins around the brake lever and climbed down from the bench. She started across the trampled grass toward the circle of children, her skirts brushing the foot-high wildflowers.

"Lookit, Miss Constance." Jamie Ramsey thrust a handful of buttercups at her.

"Why, they're lovely, Jamie. Won't your mother be pleased?"

"Ain't for Momma, they're for you! My momma says you'n your sister are brave souls."

Constance kept moving, and Jamie tagged at her

heels. "What's a brave soul? Is it like a shoe that don't wear out?"

"Mercy, no. It's…well, it's…like a *person* that doesn't wear out."

Oh, Lord, let me truly live up to Mrs. Ramsey's perception. I cannot afford to wear out. I must be strong for Nettie. I promised Papa.

She took a step forward and Nettie whirled toward her, a triumphant smile on her face. "Cissy, you'll never guess what they're saying!"

"You should not be listening," she said in an undertone. Again her gaze settled on the major and Mr. Duquette, whose face had turned florid.

Nettie linked arms with her. "But it's so interesting, hearing things you're not supposed to."

Constance slid her arm around her sister's slim waist. "Hush. Don't let the children hear you, or we'll never have another moment's privacy." She swung Nettie in a half circle and drew her back toward the wagon.

Nettie rested her head briefly against her shoulder. "Don't be angry, Cissy."

"I'm not angry. I'm just doing what Papa would want me to."

"I know," she said with an aggrieved sigh. "Papa wanted me to grow up respectable." She kicked the head off a buttercup with the toe of her shoe. "And so do you."

"I want you to be happy, Nettie." She squeezed her sister's arm.

Nettie huffed and then giggled. "Oh, Cissy, just wait until I tell you what I overheard!" She walked on ahead, Ruth and Essie clinging to her hands and trailed by the three Ramsey boys.

With a wry smile, Constance noted her sister's dainty steps, the way she tossed her head and laughed. Nettie always knew when she was being watched. No one would ever suspect how she wept and complained when she was alone in the wagon at night.

Keeping her eye on Mr. Duquette, Constance unwound the reins from the brake lever and waited for the signal to move forward. When she saw the wagon leader tramping back toward the wagons, his jaw set, she knew something was wrong.

Without saying a word to anyone, he headed for the front of the line. Every time he stomped his boot down, it sent up a little puff of dust.

Gracious, what on earth had passed between Duquette and the major?

Nettie knew. But Nettie would take her time sharing the information. Withholding it made her feel important.

"Excuse me, Miss Weldon." The voice sounded so close to her elbow she jerked in surprise.

The major stood before her. His jaw looked tight, and he wasn't smiling.

"Yes?"

The instant her eyes met his the earth seemed to stop turning. All she could think of were how blue they were. Deep, dark blue, the exact shade of the bottle of writing ink Papa had kept on his desk. Her mouth was suddenly dry as an old tea towel.

"Yes?" she said again. "What is it?"

Billy West stepped his horse up on the other side of her wagon. The major gestured, and Billy trotted on after Duquette.

The longer she looked at the tall man before her, the stranger she felt, as if she was desperately treading water to keep from sinking. He had five button loops on his fawn-colored shirt, the top two unfastened.

He said nothing for a long moment. Then, "Miss Weldon, move your wagon up next to the Ramseys'."

"But Mr. Duquette told me to—"

"Next to the Ramseys'," he repeated, his voice flat. "And stay in the center position. Other wagons will flank you."

"But why?"

"It's just you and your sister, is it not?" He didn't wait for her answer. "Wagons with unattached women or children will take the center. We'll spread out, travel side by side in two ranks."

"Because?"

"Because it's safer. And there's less dust that way."

Instantly she saw the sense of it, and just as quickly wondered why Mr. Duquette had insisted on traveling single file.

The major's penetrating blue eyes held her gaze. "If you don't mind my asking, Miss Weldon, what are you and your sister doing out here alone?"

"We are not alone. There are ten other wagons."

"I meant why are just the two of you undertaking this journey?"

Constance swallowed, letting her gaze settle on Nettie, who was now playing rag-ball catch with Elijah Ramsey.

"My father wanted to settle in Oregon. But when we were all packed up and ready to leave Independence, Papa took sick and died."

"Why did you not turn back?"

Constance bit her lower lip. *How much should she tell him?*

"Papa made me promise I would take Nettie and

go on to Oregon. It was…he said it was something he had always wanted.''

"You mind telling me what business your father was in?''

The question surprised her. "He was a respected banker. Major Montgomery, why is that important now?''

"I need to know you are adequately provided for.''

"And why is that? Mr. Duquette made no such inquiries when we signed on. He asked nothing of us but his fee.''

"That figures. It's a long way to Oregon, Miss Weldon. And it's hard traveling, the worst kind. A month from now you'll think you're going to hell, not Oregon. To make it, you need adequate provisions and a good amount of cash money.''

"My father was a very careful man. He provided for us very well on both accounts.''

John studied the blue-painted wagon. It looked well built. Bigger than most. Extrawide canvas in the bonnet. Why would a careful man, a banker, want to pull up roots and head out to the frontier?

"Major Montgomery?''

He shifted his gaze to the young woman perched on the driver's bench. Shiny brown hair, the color of polished saddle leather, caught in a single thick plait down the back of her plain brown dress. Couldn't be much older than twenty-two or -three; old enough to have a husband. Children, even. The hands holding the oxen traces were slim and sun browned, and beneath the simple wide-brimmed straw, hat clear hazel eyes regarded him with wary curiosity and something else. Intelligence.

She was not pretty, exactly. More like what you'd call handsome. Something about her was very arresting, the bones of her face, maybe. And those eyes.

"Major?"

"Ma'am?"

"May I ask you a question for a change?"

"If you like."

She looked straight at him. "Why are you now giving orders instead of Mr. Duquette?"

She was direct, all right. "Army protocol," he lied. "Military escorts and scouts know more about the trail than most wagon leaders. Sometimes it saves lives."

He thought it unnecessary to explain that Duquette was so inexperienced he marveled the party had gotten this far. No need to humiliate the man. Besides, a dog that gets kicked usually bites back. He'd just make sure things went smoothly and let Duquette take the credit.

He had started to turn away when her voice stopped him. "Why do we need a military escort in the first place?"

"You're going into Indian country. Sometimes Indians object to the white man trampling all over his land."

"Oh." She cocked her head, a thoughtful look on her face. "Do Indians steal horses?"

"Some do."

"Why?"

He had to chuckle inside. She sure didn't give up easy. "Indians prize horses. They're regarded as wealth, to be traded, given as gifts, even used to buy wives."

"Buy wives?"

He ignored the comment.

"And they ride them in battle. Are you frightened, Miss Weldon?"

"Not of Indians, Major." Her tone was matter-of-fact, her gaze steady. "I fear only that we, Nettie and myself, will not reach Oregon, as Papa wanted. But I do not think Indians will be our greatest trial."

John stared at her. He couldn't help it. Hell, she talked exactly like Colonel Harry Butterworth when he had his back against the wall. A cooler man under pressure he'd never known.

But a twenty-three-year-old woman fresh from the States? That was unusual. *She* was unusual.

He turned over in his mind something Billy West had said. *"Gonna be females in that train. Pretty ones."*

Now, looking at the slim young woman before him, he heard the knowing voice of his companion in his ear. *"Told ya so."*

He lifted two fingers to his hat brim. "My compliments, ma'am." He strode toward his waiting horse.

Chapter Four

Mr. West took supper with us this evening. The major and his friend, Mr. West, will take turns eating with the Ollesen brothers and with us, so as not to be a burden.

To stretch our dwindling supply of food, I added some molasses and a bit of mustard to the beans and made an extra pan of johnnycake. Mrs. Ramsey sent over a dried apple pie; I do wonder how she finds the time to bake with a new baby to care for! Elijah brought the pie and stayed for supper, too. Nettie taught him to spell apple.

Mr. West is a pleasant, friendly sort of man, with a great store of adventures to recount. He told us about the time he and Major John (that is what he calls Major Montgomery when he is not within hearing) were chased by a grizzly bear. I thought Elijah's eyes would pop out!

After Mr. West left, Nettie confessed what she had overheard between the major and Mr. Duquette, and it was this: Major Montgomery has lived among the Indians! I told her I did not find that surprising, as I understand from Mr. West that many Indian agents and trappers and others have done so.

But Nettie found it quite intriguing and pestered Mr. West for the details. He told her it was "none of your concern." I quite like his forthright manner. Nettie, however, went off to bed in a fluff.

Tomorrow night we will have the major to supper. Whatever shall we eat, besides beans?

"Cissy, my shoes are wearing through!" Nettie stood off to one side of the rolling wagon, one foot raised, peering at the sole of her leather walking boot.

"You could drive the team if you'd rather," Constance offered. "I will walk."

Nettie grimaced. "No, I'd rather not. It's too jouncy on that hard bench. Doesn't your...don't you get numb?"

Constance grinned at her sister. "How I wish! At least then I wouldn't feel every bump and rut on this prairie."

Nettie resumed her quick steps through the cluster

of children at her skirts, and Constance heard her voice float above the creak of wagon wheels.

"Now, Jamie, it's your turn. Can you think of five words that start with the letter *b?*"

They had already been through the alphabet once. Now the game would start over. She did admire her sister's perseverance with the children, even though Nettie complained constantly about being too tired to help with the camp chores. The game passed the time while the wagons crunched over the grassy plain and Nettie and the children trudged alongside. Soon, Constance realized, they would *all* have holes in their shoes, and then what?

Seven-year-old Jamie pursed his lips in concentration. "Um...*barrel.* And *bird.*" He frowned. "And...*Billy?* Does a name count?"

At Nettie's nod, he continued. *"Board."* And... lessee, uh...*battlefield!* I learned that from Mr. West."

"Oh, never mind that," Nettie said quickly. "That's just men talk. Now, what words begin with the letter *c?* Ruth? Essie?"

Constance let her thoughts wander to the coming evening, when the major would join them for supper. She had thought about it all day. They were low on meat, but there was some bacon left, and she had enough flour to make extra biscuits. And—she strained her eyes past the lead wagon—maybe there would be some wild berry bushes ahead.

And oh, please, a stream. She did long to wash the dust out of her hair. Nettie brushed a handful of cornmeal through her hair every night, but Constance didn't want to dip further into their larder if she could avoid it.

The major rode behind the wagons, back far enough to avoid the fine dust kicked up by hooves and wagon wheels, but not so distant that Constance couldn't observe him whenever she twisted her head.

He sat straight-spined in the saddle, but he moved with the shiny black mare in an easy, loose-jointed way that made her shiver. It was beautiful to watch, as if the horse and the dark-haired man were somehow connected. As if they *liked* each other.

She let her gaze settle on Nettie, stepping along inside the gaggle of young ones that danced about her. Like a queen and her retinue. When one of the Ramsey children felt uneasy around someone, they walked stiff-jointed, their shoulders rigid. Around Nettie, they frolicked like floppy rag dolls.

Again she glanced back at the tall man following on horseback. The major looked relaxed. It was only when he spoke to her that his body seemed to tighten.

Well, she did have that effect on males. The young men in Liberty Corners hadn't liked her much. Too outspoken, they said. Too independent. Well, she hadn't much liked them, either.

The thought of "the spinster sister" surreptitiously watching a man brought a wry smile to her lips. This man wasn't like any of those in Liberty Corners, but he was very definitely male, and males just…well, they just didn't like her.

And no amount of fluffy biscuits and crisp bacon would make a teaspoon's worth of difference.

"Is he here yet?" Nettie whispered from the back of the wagon.

Constance mopped her perspiring cheeks and forehead with her apron. "Not yet. He stopped to talk to Mr. Ramsey." She slid the second pan of biscuits out of the makeshift oven she'd set over the iron grate. Bacon strips sizzled in the skillet.

"Hurry and fetch the plates, Nettie."

"Just a minute," her sister called. She ducked back inside the bonnet and Constance heard the unmistakable sound of humming, punctuated by something clicking onto a wooden surface. The hairbrush. Nettie brushed her hair one hundred strokes each and every day.

"Now, Nettie. The major is heading this way."

Nettie floated down from the wagon. A blue ribbon secured the silvery-blond hair at her neck, and she wore the clean blouse Constance was saving for Sunday. And she smelled of lilac scent!

Oh, how could *she? I smell of wood smoke and bacon drippings.* Her apron was spotted, and she was so hot and sticky she'd undone the top two buttons of her dress and hadn't time—or hands clean enough—to close them up.

Nettie looked rested and fresh. *She* herself must look like she'd been rolled in the dirt.

The major strode into the firelight. "Evening, Miss Weldon."

She kept her back to him. She opened her mouth to reply, then heard Nettie's soft voice.

"Good evening, Major. Won't you join us? Supper is almost ready."

"Thank you, I will." But he stood at the edge of their camp as if waiting for something.

Constance busied herself piling the biscuits into a bowl and checking the butter supply. Plenty for supper, but tomorrow she'd have to churn again.

Nettie swished past her. "Sit right here, Major Montgomery, and I'll bring you a plate. Would you prefer coffee or tea?"

"Coffee, if you have enough."

"Why, of course we do," Nettie trilled. "We have plenty of everything."

"Nettie." Constance worked to keep her voice even. They had exactly one handful of coffee beans to last them to Fort Kearny, where they could replenish their supplies.

Her sister raised wide blue eyes. "What?"

Constance sighed. Nettie excelled at Pretend. That was one of the reasons the children adored her. Nettie was…creative.

"Nothing. Be sure to shake the dust out of the coffee mill."

The major rose from the canvas seat he'd taken. "I'll grind it. Where's the mill?"

His eyes met hers and for a split second everything around them—the bacon crackling in the pan, Molly bawling from the Ollesen's rope corral, a baby squalling—came to a hushed stop.

"On a p-peg just inside the wagon."

Nettie jumped up. "I'll show you." The set of her jaw dared Constance to object.

Major Montgomery held up his hand. "No need. If I remember right, I banged my head on it when young Cal and I were having our 'discussion.'"

Constance began forking the bacon onto a platter. "The beans are in the canister on the lower shelf."

The major stalked past her to the rear of the

wagon, and in a moment she heard the crunch and rattle of the coffee grinder.

Nettie leaned forward, her gaze on the wagon. "Will there be enough?" she whispered.

"I'll have tea," Constance whispered back. "Here, load up the major's plate. I'll put the water on to boil."

The major rejoined the circle to find the younger sister staring at him with a triumphant smile on her face, the older bent over the cook fire with her back to him. He reached around her and dumped the scant box of ground coffee into the smoke-blackened pot she pointed out.

"Thank you," she murmured.

Her voice went through him like a sharpened saber. Something about it, the clear, resonant tone maybe, or the fact that she didn't look up as he moved near her, made him pause.

She was not afraid of him, not awed by authority the way the younger sister was. This one, Constance, was shy around men. Or maybe just around him.

She all but ignored him as she went about the business of serving up supper. Nettie, he noted, hovered near, shifting from one foot to the other as if she couldn't decide where to settle. Constance was surefooted, her movements steady as she focused on what she was doing.

The curious tension in his gut began to ease.

Nettie alighted finally and patted the camp chair beside her. "Major Montgomery," she purred. "Do sit here by me."

There were only two seats. If he took the one offered, Constance would have to sit on the ground.

"It might be more comfortable—"

"Why, Major, you are our guest! I *order* you—" a giggle escaped "—to keep me company. Besides, Cissy prefers the ground. Don't you, Cissy?"

Nettie leaned toward him. "She says it's cooler," she confided in an undertone. "Cissy even sleeps on the ground, underneath the wagon."

"It *is* cooler," Constance said. She crossed her feet and sank onto the folded blanket that served as their table, patted down her skirt and settled a plate of beans and biscuits on her lap. Mercy, Nettie was a chatterbox tonight. Worse than last night with Mr. West.

She raised her fork, then lowered it thoughtfully. Well, of course she was! Nettie was lonely. They'd left everyone they knew in Liberty Corners—the governess, Miss Grandet, Cook and every last one of Nettie's beaux. Not one thing was known and familiar now except for Molly the cow and the wagon load of Mama's furniture. No wonder Nettie was hungry for company.

The major forked up beans and bacon and listened to Nettie explain the games she made up for the children. He answered her sister's questions in his low, steady voice, but he was watching *her*.

Her heart doubled a beat.

Suddenly Nettie's voice rose in a calculated wail. "But why, Major?" The wheedling tone jerked Constance to attention.

"Please," Nettie wheedled. "I won't tell anyone."

"Nettie," she cautioned. "It isn't polite to pry."

The major rose, poured himself a cup of the hot coffee and stood looking down on them. "No harm done," he said. He caught Constance's gaze and held it. "Your sister is naturally curious."

Curious! The major was no fool; he was covering up Nettie's bad manners.

"Thanks for supper, Miss Weldon. And for the coffee." He raised the speckled tin cup in a salute and turned to leave.

"There's dessert," Constance offered. "Blackberries I picked this afternoon."

He didn't respond. Instead, he walked out of the firelight and headed away from the wagon circle. "I'll bring the cup back later," he said over his shoulder.

Nettie leaped to her feet and stared after him. "Well, I never!" she blurted.

"You overstepped, Sister. Leave him alone."

"Mr. West said he does the same thing every night, just walks off into the dark. Don't you think it odd?"

"Not in the slightest. We've nothing to look at all day but the same flat plain and the same wagons, the same faces. Nothing to hear but wheels thumping and Mrs. Ramsey's baby crying. Why wouldn't a person want a few moments of peace and quiet?"

Nettie fisted her hands on her hips. "I don't understand you, Cissy. Not at all. Don't you simply *long* to know things about people? Secret things?"

Constance surveyed her sister. With her silvery hair and pale skin, she was like a moonbeam. It was hard for her to keep still for any length of time, hard for her to focus her mind on one thing long enough to truly comprehend it.

And, she acknowledged with a sigh, it was hard, terribly hard, for Nettie to feel left out of anything.

"Yes, I long to know things about people. Some people, that is. I long to be close enough to another human being that I will not need to ask about their thoughts or feelings, for I will know them instinctively."

Nettie's lips pushed into a pout. "Well, then?"

"But not a man's secrets. Those I would wish to know only if he chose to tell me. I would not wish to gain such knowledge without his wanting me to know."

Nettie looked down at her shoes. "Nor should I, I suppose."

"Nor should you." She gave her sister a quick hug. "Now, help me wash up the plates, and let's forget all about secrets and such. And the *next* time Major Montgomery comes to supper…"

"Oh, yes, Cissy, I know. Don't pry." She turned her back.

"But I still want to know," she said under her breath.

Chapter Five

Nettie pleaded a headache and climbed into the wagon for the night, and Constance washed and dried the tin supper plates and shoveled dirt over the fire pit. She was bending to tidy up the pantry box when she remembered the blackberries.

Heaped in a speckled bowl, they beckoned from the top of the wooden shelf where she had set them before supper. She gazed at the shiny blue-black fruit, and her mouth watered.

She tasted one. The sweet juice exploded on her tongue, and she closed her eyes in delight.

"Nettie," she called. "Would you like some blackberries?"

No answer. She poked her head through the canvas bonnet. "Nettie?" she whispered. "Are you awake?"

She listened hard but heard only the snores of Mr. Nyland two wagons away and the far-off cry of a coyote. The breeze sighed across the darkened land, and Constance looked up at the star-spangled sky arching overhead. In the face of such vastness, her small daily concerns were insignificant. *How puny our eleven wagons are compared with the unending plain, the rivers we must cross, the strength of the sun and the wind.*

All at once the taste of that sweet, ripe blackberry seemed the most important thing on earth. Quickly she piled a handful each in two small bowls and set out in the direction the major had gone.

The night air was soft and warm and full of cricket calls. She walked gingerly, feeling her way until her eyes adjusted to the dark. It took some minutes until she finally caught sight of him, and when she did, she stopped short.

He stood a good distance from the circle of wagons, facing away from her. One hand rested on his hip, the other held the cup of coffee he'd poured after supper, but he wasn't drinking it. His face was tilted up, looking at the sky.

She moved toward him, her skirt swishing over the grass. The major half turned toward her, and in silence she handed him one bowl of berries. He accepted it without speaking.

She selected a berry from her own bowl, closed her lips over it and crushed it against the roof of her mouth with her tongue. The taste was so exquisitely delicious it made her cheeks ache.

She ate another, held the juice in her mouth as long as she could before swallowing. Then she scooped up a whole handful and gobbled them down.

The major tipped the container to his lips and shook some into his mouth. She nibbled her berries, watching him from time to time out of the corner of her eye, until their bowls were empty.

Without a word, he flung the remains of his coffee onto the ground, lifted the empty bowl out of her hand and set it inside his own. He gave her a long look, and she thought she saw the faint shadow of a smile touch his lips.

He turned away once more and tipped his head back to study the canopy of winking diamonds spread above them. How serene and quiet the universe was. It made the searing heat of the day, the wearying miles of travel seem unimportant. *There is meaning and purpose in this life, even if I cannot fathom what it might be.*

She turned the puzzling thought over in her mind until she gradually became aware of the man beside her, his breathing slow and measured. The heat emanating from his body, the faint odor of dust and sweat and coffee stopped her heartbeat for an instant. She sneaked a glance at him.

His eyes were closed, but he lifted his face to the sky and inhaled, exhaled, inhaled, almost as if waiting for something. And then he opened his eyelids and turned to look at her.

She sucked in her breath at what she saw. He blinked, but not before she saw the moisture that shone in his eyes. Then he looked beyond her, into the darkness, and again the ghost of a smile crossed his face. It was gone so quickly she wondered if she had imagined it.

At the same instant they turned back toward the flickering campfires within the wagon circle. Their steps matched.

For hours she lay awake on her pallet under the wagon, remembering the unguarded expression in the major's eyes, thinking about her reaction. Perhaps Papa had been right: there were things about life she had not yet learned.

When the stars faded and the sky began to turn gray, she dozed off, only to be jolted awake by an angry shout.

"Gotdammit, two more horses we haf stolen!"

"Quick, fetch Mr. Duquette!" Arvo's voice.

"Better Major Montgomery," Cal yelled. "He knows more about..."

The rest of his words were obliterated by Molly's bawling to be milked and Mrs. Nyland's rooster noisily announcing sunup.

It couldn't be morning already! Her limbs felt as if they were made of lead. With an effort, Constance rolled out from under the wagon. Her arms, her shoulders, even her ribs ached. The thought of driving the team another fifteen miles brought tears to her eyes. She couldn't. She just couldn't.

She commanded her body into an upright position and dragged herself into the wagon to dress. Nettie would have to drive. It was time she shared more of the work.

"Wake up, Nettie."

Her sister turned over and curled into a lump under the quilt.

"Nettie. Please."

Constance stared at her sleeping sister. All of a sudden she wanted to scream. She bit her tongue until the urge passed, then splashed her face with cool water from the using bucket she'd filled the evening before.

The only looking glass was atop Mama's mahogany chiffonier, but she avoided it, preferring to comb and rebraid her hair by feel. Who cared what she looked like out here, hundreds of miles from Logan County?

She froze with the hairbrush poised above her head. Up until this morning, the loose, untidy braid had served. She knew her eyes were swollen from lack of sleep, her freckles darker because of the sun beating down on them all day. Her teeth felt furry, and her fingernails...

She lowered the brush, glanced down at her hand and snapped her eyes shut. Her nails were broken and uneven, her hands and face tanned the color of saddle leather. Oh, wouldn't the women back in Liberty Corners have things to say about that!

Connie, dear, what have *you done to your hair?*

And your freckles! Oh, you poor bedraggled thing...

Poor bedraggled thing? Merciful heaven, if she didn't stop such thinking she would end up as vain as Nettie. Not once in the past three hundred miles had she spared a single thought for her appearance. Until now.

Now there was...

Outside the wagon came the pounding of horses' hooves and a taut voice. "Put down that rifle, you damn fool!"

Constance dropped the hairbrush as if it were a

hot coal. "Nettie, wake up! It's morning," she hissed.

She pulled her dress on over her petticoat and buttoned it up as she stepped out of the wagon.

Joshua Duquette stood spraddle-legged over her cooking pit, a rifle pointed at the major, who was mounted on his dark mare. "Get outta my way."

"Put the gun down, Duquette. They're long gone by now."

"It's Indians, ain't it?" Duquette spit. *"Ain't it?"*

The major pointed at the rifle, and the grumbling wagon leader swung the barrel to one side.

"I said lower it," the major snapped. "You want to accidentally kill one of your own party?"

"I know how to handle a gun, Major."

"I've seen women handle firearms better than you do."

Constance gasped. Women? He knew women—a woman—who could shoot a gun?

Duquette pointed the rifle at the ground. "Is it Indians or not, Major?"

"Probably."

"Then why cain't I shoot 'em?"

The major crossed his wrists on the pommel and leaned forward. "Because they're not here. And you don't want to hunt for them. They know this country better than you do."

"So just what are we s'posed to do?"

The major straightened in the saddle. "Best if we get moving. Keep a sharp lookout and keep the wagons rolling."

"And then what?" Duquette snarled.

"Wait until dark. An Indian won't steal a horse in broad daylight. Not if he has a choice."

A shiver went up Constance's spine. While she had tossed on her pallet, thinking about the major, someone—an Indian—had sneaked into camp, *walked right past her lying beneath the wagon* and spirited away two more of the Ollesen's mares. *Why hadn't she heard anything?*

She shuddered. She didn't want to admit it, but she was frightened. And Nettie…merciful heaven, her sister would be beside herself! She prayed that Nettie still slept, that she hadn't heard the commotion outside the wagon.

To be honest, she envied Nettie's ability to slide away from things she didn't want to think about. Nettie addressed herself only to what suited her at the moment.

She hated to admit it, but her sister's weepy self-absorption was getting harder and harder to swallow. Nettie was not pulling her weight.

Mr. Duquette and the major moved apart, Duquette heading back to the lead wagon, the major…well, Constance didn't know where he was going. Where, she wondered, had he slept last night?

Mrs. Ramsey's baby began to cry, and a sliver of red-gold sun peeped over the edge of the plain. By the time she had milked Molly and set the milk pans to rise, Nettie began to stir.

She heard the splash of water, the swish-swish of the hairbrush, and then the clunk of a shoe on the wood wagon bed. Automatically Constance bent to prepare their breakfast of leftover biscuits and tea, and then suddenly straightened. Today she would insist that Nettie share more of the work.

She hated to do it. Nettie was delicate and moody, still grieving for Papa.

Well, so was she! Besides, in the long run it was for Nettie's own good. From now on, life would be far harsher than their genteel, pampered existence in Ohio.

Oh, how she longed to be away from all this! Safe and warm and…and cared about. When evening came, she would walk off by herself and have a good cry.

"Wait until dark," the major had said. And then what?

Would he walk out to look at the stars tonight, with Indians around?

* * *

Billy West reined in his mount and waited to see what the major had on his mind. From the look on his face—one he recognized from years of campaigning together—it wasn't good news. He shoved his hat back.

"What's up, John?"

"Stolen horses."

"Told 'ya so. How many?"

"Two more."

"Doesn't sound like Cheyenne. Hell, they'd take everything on four legs but the cow."

Montgomery said nothing. Billy waited until he thought he'd pop.

"'Member the time up in the Yaak River country when we—"

"Yep."

"Been thinkin' what I'm thinkin'?"

"Yep."

"So, what you gonna do this time, John?"

The major gave him another look Billy had come to know.

"Lay a trap."

Chapter Six

Near midnight the breeze dropped to a soft breath across John's face. In the quiet, every sound was audible—the snap of a twig, a birdcall, even the breathing of the two horses he'd picketed a short distance from the wagons. A thieving Cheyenne would be tempted by such easy pickings.

A dozen yards away he knew Billy West also waited, concealed behind a fallen cottonwood with his Winchester across his knees. Neither man had as much as twitched a little finger for the past three hours. The last time he and Billy had staked out a horse thief, he'd worked his way halfway through Genesis from memory. Tonight it was songs. "My Bonnie Lies Over the Ocean." "Polly Wolly Doodle." "Shenandoah." Another hour alone with his thoughts would be more than he could stomach.

He checked his pocket for the extra box of cartridges and hoped Billy had done the same. Maybe the setup wouldn't work this time. They would both be firing at the same target from opposite sides of the decoy; he hated the thought of a shot going wild.

He heard a faint click behind the horses. Not a footstep. Billy's teeth snapping shut? The safety catch on a rifle? The hair on his neck prickled.

There it was again. John had to smile. It wasn't the quietest Indian he'd ever heard.

Another click, and then a swishing sound. Maybe not an Indian. More like a...

A single whippoorwill call floated out of the dark. Billy. He cupped his hands to answer.

John held his breath. If it wasn't Billy, and it wasn't an Indian, that meant someone or something unexpected was out there in the dark with them.

He signaled again. This time the whipporwill call came from farther to the right. Billy was moving.

Something scraped against a stone. John eased the rifle into position and stared into the blackness.

A flicker of something light colored caught his eye, and he shifted the barrel an inch to the left. The murmur of the stream suddenly seemed loud enough to wake the entire camp.

Just beyond the horses he heard a snuffling noise. Very carefully John rose to a standing position, the rifle butt braced against his shoulder. Straining his eyes into the dark, he waited.

A figure stepped into his sights, and John blinked and refocused. A woman. Her skirt swaying, she sidestepped the two horses and headed straight toward the stream bank, swiping at her eyes with one hand.

Lord God Almighty. Constance Weldon. What in the hell…?

She carried something in her other hand. As she drew closer, he saw what it was—a loaf of bread. Fresh baked, from the fragrant smell of it. As she walked, she pinched a piece from it and stuffed it into her mouth.

What was she doing out here? He lowered the rifle, leaned it against his thigh and again cupped his hands, but before he could signal Billy, an Indian stepped out of the deep shadows directly in her path.

John's heart rose into his throat.

She stopped short, one hand at her mouth. *Don't move!* he ordered silently. Sweat started under his hat brim.

To her credit she didn't scream. The Cheyenne and the woman stared at each other for maybe a full minute.

That's the way, lady. Don't move. And don't talk.

Constance felt her heart hammer against her corset stays. *He will hear it,* she thought irrationally. *He will know I am afraid.*

The man's gaze dropped from her face to her hands and a harsh breath rasped in. She took in his ragged shirt, the dust-caked bandanna knotted around his forehead. *An Indian.* Thank heaven Nettie was safe in the wagon.

She struggled to steady her breathing. *He is looking at my hands. He must see that I am not armed.*

The Indian glided forward a step and studied her face again. His eyes were dark. Wary. He wanted something. On impulse, she thrust the bread toward him.

He stared at her for a moment longer, then snatched it out of her fingers so deftly she barely felt it. She noticed his arm was twisted at the elbow.

He tore at the loaf, wolfing down mouthfuls while his black eyes remained on her. All at once he grasped her wrist in his sinewy fingers. She opened her mouth to scream, but no sound came out. His fingers tightened, tugged her forward. *Oh God, he was going to kill her.*

And then a voice came out of the dark. "She is not for you, Brother."

The Indian dropped her wrist and spun toward the sound.

Major Montgomery stepped out of the shadows

and moved unhurriedly to her side. The Indian's eyes followed his every step. Constance was dizzy with relief.

The major raised his hand. "Yellow Wolf, do you now steal horses and women?"

"Brother," the Indian replied. "I greet you."

"Answer my question."

The Indian shrugged. "You know the answer."

"I do," the major acknowledged. "I have been waiting for you."

"And I, you." He gestured at the two horses. "I will not take the horse my father gave to you, nor the spotted one belonging to Billy West."

The major nodded. "Wagon master reports three mares missing."

"I steal to eat. Your horse I will not take." He took a step toward Constance. "But I will have this woman."

Constance felt the major's hand at her back, a gentle pressure that told her to say nothing. She stifled an urge to laugh. As if she could speak a single syllable with terror turning her tongue into a frozen lump.

"This woman belongs to me," the major said in a low voice.

"I do not believe you."

"Believe. In this, I do not lie."

"And Little Star?"

The hand at her back jerked. "Little Star is dead."

"Yes. You are not lucky with women, John. When my belly cried out, this one offered bread. Take care that you do not harm her."

"I will not harm her."

"I will be watching."

"As will I."

The Indian raised his crooked arm. "Be well, Brother. And do not forget."

"And you, Yellow Wolf. I forget nothing."

The Indian turned and melted into the night. Constance stood rooted until the major lifted his hand from her back, and then her knees buckled. She stumbled forward, and he caught her shoulders in his strong warm hands.

"Steady," he murmured. "It's all over. You did well." Then he gave her a little shake. "But what the *hell* are you doing out here?"

"I—I was…upset." Her voice sounded odd. Tight. "Nettie and I had words before supper, and I set some bread to rise to take my mind off the matter. After supper I was still upset, so I baked the bread and went for a walk."

John said nothing.

"That Indian, Yellow Wolf you called him?"

The major's hands tightened about her shoulders. "What about him?"

She wanted to know a thousand things. Why did they address each other as "brother?" Who was Little Star? But something stopped her. Major Montgomery valued his privacy. She sensed he had already revealed more of himself than he'd wanted. She would ask him nothing personal.

"Did…did he really want to claim me as his woman?"

The major released her. "He wanted you, all right. You offered him food. To a starving Indian, that's a powerful incentive. Your gesture spoke louder than any words."

He shot her a keen look. "Why does that surprise you?"

Constance hesitated. "I have never been… wanted." In the next instant found the words locked in her heart tumbling willy-nilly past her lips.

"No one ever has before. Wanted me, I mean. Not in Logan County."

"Were there no young men in Logan County?"

"Oh yes. But…" Her voice dropped to a whisper. "But they didn't want me for *me*. They never really knew who I was, inside. And Papa, too. Papa needed me to keep house and care for Nettie after Mama died."

He gave her a steady look. "Yellow Wolf doesn't know you, either, but he'll want what you offer. Keep that in mind, Miss Weldon."

"Is that all men ever want?" she blurted. "What a woman can *do* for them? Feed them and wash their clothes and…"

"Some men, yes."

"What about the others?" Her heart thumped against her stays. "You, for instance?"

"A man who doesn't see what else you've got to offer besides good biscuits and clean shirts is blind."

"Oh," Constance breathed. *Oh.* Did that mean he liked her? Approved of her just as she was? With her hair all which-a-way and her skin smelling of wood smoke?

"You don't think I am too…" How did Papa put it? "Outspoken?"

"Some women are quiet. Others aren't. Nothing wrong with speaking out in most circumstances." He studied her with eyes that pierced right through her.

Too smart for your own good, Papa had said. *Ought to be softer, like Nettie. It's honey that catches a husband, not vinegar.*

Maybe she didn't *want* to catch herself a husband. Men were…well, men were men.

"Unless you want to get carried off by a renegade Cheyenne, I wouldn't walk beyond the wagon perimeter at night."

"I don't like people telling me what I can and cannot do, Major."

"I'm not 'people,' Miss Weldon. I'm your military escort." He took her elbow and spoke into the dark.

"Can you hear me, Billy?"

"I hear you," came a raspy voice some distance away.

"Take the horses to the Ollesen's corral. I'm going to walk Miss Weldon back to camp."

"Which one?" came the voice. "There's two Miss Weldons. The pretty one or the other one?"

Constance bit her lip.

"Goddammit," the major said under his breath. "Shut your trap, Billy."

"Yessir, Major. Right away. Guess yer testy temper tells me which one."

The major turned her toward camp. "Come on."

"I don't like men—majors or military escorts—telling me what to do, either."

He kept on walking. "That so."

It wasn't a question. What came out of his mouth sounded as if it didn't matter in the least what she liked or did not like.

"To my mind," he said in an even voice, "there's a big difference between independent minded and cantankerous."

"There's also a big difference between 'the pretty one' and 'the other one,'" she blurted.

"Sure is." His voice sounded like he was swallowing a chuckle. She yanked her elbow out of his grasp.

"You bake bread often?"

Now where had *that* come from? The man changed subjects so fast she was always off balance.

"I bake every third day. Every other day I churn butter."

"An extra loaf left on a rock or in the crook of a tree now and again might be welcome in some quarters."

She noticed he had carefully worded the statement so it could not be taken as telling her what to do. She had to smile. "Major, are you suggesting…?"

"Nope. Just making an observation."

Behind them came the faint *tap-tap* of a picket peg being pulled up. A horse whinnied, and a gruff male voice—Billy West, she assumed—uttered soothing noises. They sounded like the nonsense syllables one gurgled to a baby. Like the words Papa had crooned over Nettie's cradle when she was an infant.

The memory brought tears to her eyes. *Papa. Oh, Papa, I am so lost and alone without you.*

Her vision blurred and she stumbled over a patch of dockweed.

"Miss Weldon?" The major caught her arm, steadied her with his strong, warm hand.

"S-sorry," she murmured. "It's hard to see."

He pulled her around to face him. "What's wrong?"

Everything, she wanted to tell him. Nettie and the scorched supper biscuits and the hollow ache in her chest and…Nettie.

"Nothing. I am a bit tired this evening. My head hurts, and—"

"Tell your sister she's not going to survive out here if she doesn't pull more of the load. Neither one of you will."

Constance gaped at him. "Why, whatever gave you the idea…"

"Tell her." He gave her shoulders a little shake. "You go on doing her share of the work and you'll die of exhaustion before you reach Fort Benton."

She looked up into an implacable face—jaw tense, lips firmed into a thin line, eyes hard as a frozen turquoise lake. She couldn't lie to him. As hard as it was to face the truth, she wanted to speak

of what was real. She opened her mouth and pro-
nounced a single word.

"Frightened."

Oh, it felt so good to let it out! Instantly she felt
better. Lighter, as if a stone pressing on her heart
had suddenly sprouted wings and flown away.

"Frightened," he echoed. "Of what? Indians?
Going hungry? Losing your oxen?" He waited, his
breath pulling in and out, his hands cupping her
shoulders. He smelled of smoke and leather, of coffee, of…something like cinnamon.

"I am afraid…" *Of what?*

She didn't know. She sucked in a breath. "I am
afraid of Nettie." The words came out in a rush. "I
mean, I am afraid *for* Nettie."

"Yes," he said. She waited for more but heard
only the *chirrup* of crickets.

"No," she heard herself whisper. "I was right the
first time. I am afraid *of* Nettie. My own sister. God
help me, I must be going crazy."

The major dropped his hands. "No, you're not
going crazy. Your sister bears watching." Again he
touched her elbow and turned her toward camp.

She had to take two steps to every one of his. "I
don't know why I said that, about my sister, I
mean."

"Not surprising," he replied. "But since you did say it, it's no doubt true on some level."

Constance shrank inside herself. "You must consider me a silly, fuddle-headed female."

"Not hardly, Miss Weldon. I think you're smarter than you think. Outspoken, as you said. It suits you. Ought to do more of it."

More of it? More of the very thing that had scared off half the young men in Logan County? At least the half that hadn't fallen under Nettie's spell.

"It doesn't…scare you?"

"Nothing a woman does is ever going to scare me," he said quickly.

"Perhaps I am jealous of Nettie," she murmured.

The major snorted. "Not likely."

"Why not? Every man who lays eyes on her is smitten. It's been that way since she turned fourteen."

"Not every man." The major lengthened his stride as they neared the circle of flickering light cast by campfires. "Good night, Miss Weldon. If you have a rifle, I'd sleep with it near you."

He was gone before she could open her mouth, striding away toward the Ollesen wagon in that purposeful, loose-limbed gait she had come to recognize.

Constance swallowed over a lump the size of her

fist. *Was* she jealous of Nettie? Because Papa had petted and spoiled her younger sister while Constance was busy feeding her and washing clothes when she might have been turning into a woman?

Perhaps just a tiny bit. She loved Nettie. Yes, she could be irritating. Selfish, even. And of course she resented their father's doting over her, but Constance knew Papa had loved her as well. There was no shortage of love in his household. Besides, she had long since recognized how unsettled she could be by Nettie's moods. Nettie's demands.

Well, then, if I am not jealous, and I am not just tired and worried, might it have something to do with the major?

Chapter Seven

The major smoothed his palm against the warm hide of his mare, now safely enclosed in the makeshift rope corral Arvo Ollesen had rigged inside the wagon circle. The Ollesen brothers had lost five of their mares since they entered Nebraska Territory. John would bet a month's pay that Yellow Wolf had all five animals holed up in a box canyon somewhere. Another eight or ten head and the wily Cheyenne could buy himself whatever he wanted. Food. Whiskey. Guns. Maybe even a wife.

Anything except his honor. That was gone forever. Even in his own tribe, the name Yellow Wolf brought a growl of disgust.

He wondered why the Indian had been left free to forage for himself on the plains. Why the Sioux, who held no Cheyenne to be honorable, hadn't killed him.

Or maybe a Sioux war party was headed this way and the ostracized Cheyenne warrior would sell them information for a sack of corn and some jerked venison.

"Gonna bed down somewhere's near tonight?" Billy West rasped at his elbow. "Don't spose you'd much want to cozy up too close to Yellow Wolf."

"Nope."

"'Member the time down in the Red Hills when you'n him fought it out over—"

"Nope. I try not to remember some things."

"You cripple up his arm like that, John?"

"No. A bullet did that."

Billy glanced up with interest. "Yours?"

John looked away. "Had it been mine, I wouldn't have missed." He gave the mare a final stroke and turned toward the corral entrance. "Let's get some sleep, old friend. Tomorrow I want you to ride point and keep a sharp eye out."

Billy pulled his frame upright. "I ain't so old, John. By my math'matical reckoning, I'm still under forty."

"Not by much, I'd guess. You've got sun-squint lines like dry ravines, and a ground blizzard caught in your beard." John hid the grin of pleasure he always felt when he and Billy needled each other.

"Huh! Sure would like to know when I was born,

though. What day and which month, I mean. I never know when to celebrate my birthday.''

''You're too far gone for birthday celebrations.''

Billy yanked off his cap. ''My hair's still black, though. I notice you're gettin' some salt in yours, Major.''

He thumb-stroked his chin. ''Think I should shave off my beard?''

John surveyed the man who'd ridden at his side for the past eighteen years. ''What the hell for?''

His scout's left eyelid closed. Tipping his head sideways he gazed at John with the quizzical expression he'd come to call Billy's ''befuddled look.''

''So's I kin be pretty, like you,'' Billy snapped. ''So Miss Weldon'll notice what a good-lookin' fella I am.''

The chuckle escaped before John could catch it. ''Her eyesight's better than that, Billy.''

Billy's eye snapped open. ''Don't josh me none, Major. I'm plumb serious. Bet you didn't know I got an eye for pretty ladies.''

This time John laughed aloud. ''Billy, you're a damn fool.''

''I ain't neither! That just proves you don't know nothin' about me. Nothin' at all.''

''I know you better than your momma did. You're

crotchety in the spring, mad about everything in the fall, mean tempered in the summer, and somnambulant all winter. And you never looked twice at any female taller than your knee.''

Billy's eyes lit up. "What's Sam Bullet mean?''

"Sleepy. You damn near hibernate all winter.''

"Hell if I do! Winter's when we dragged that supply wagon outta Smoky Hill Canyon, 'member, John? I do lotsa things in the winter. Why, I remember the time up in Idaho when we—''

John clapped his friend on the shoulder. "Sure, shave off your beard, Billy. Might keep your jaw from flapping. Now, Mr. West, it's Sam Bullet time, so let's…''

Billy checked the picket rope on his pinto. "Know what your problem is, Major?''

"Yep.''

"You got yourself detoured from life.''

"Yep.''

"You oughta notice pretty ladies, John. Do you a world of good.''

John bit back the retort that curled around his tongue. Billy was just trying to help, making small talk so he wouldn't have to think too much about Yellow Wolf and…other things.

"I'm sure Miss Constance will admire you without your beard, Billy.''

"Miss Constance! Who said anything about Miss Constance? I meant Miss Nettie. She's a firecracker, she is."

"Firecracker," John repeated. "You sure you don't have them mixed up?"

"Naw. I been studyin' them two sisters." Billy crossed one foot over the other and grasped his unbuttoned leather vest with both hands, as if preparing to give a speech.

"You have, have you?" John didn't want to hear one word of Billy's long-winded analyses. Especially not after seeing how upset Constance was about her younger sister. He didn't want to think about Constance Weldon one minute longer than absolutely necessary.

But for some reason he couldn't make his legs move him toward the corral gate.

"Miss Nettie, now, she's like a flea on a hot skillet. Skittish, like. And none too straightforward, neither. What she needs is a firm hand to steady her down and keep her on the straight."

John nodded. For all of Billy's reticence around women, he had the keen eye of a man who saw right through most people. Even females. He was faintly relieved that Billy wasn't blinded by the younger sister's silver-spun hair and pouting lips. Billy saw what there was to see—an attractive but self-

centered young woman with more glitter than backbone. Sand, his father had called it.

"Want me to tell ya 'bout Miss Constance?" His
friend spread his arms in a gesture John recognized.
His sermon stance.

"No, I don't," he said quickly.

"How come, Major? You got her all figured out
already?"

Figured out? A man didn't "figure out" a woman
like Constance Weldon in a few days. Or a few
months. Women like Constance took years, maybe
an entire lifetime to really understand. His mother
had been such a woman. Pa had never figured out
the first thing about her beyond the fact that she was
a general's daughter and ended up being a general's
wife who carried out her duties to perfection. What
was underneath, his father had never cared to find
out.

"Now you take Miss Constance," Billy began.
"Bein' the older sister—"

"I'm not interested." John stalked out of the corral, grabbed the bedroll he'd stashed in the back of
Ollesens' wagon and headed for the spreading cottonwood grove on the other side of camp.

Billy did the same but went on talking. "There's
trouble comin' between those two. I seed that right
off."

John jerked the rawhide strap around his rolled-up quilt and underblanket and flapped the pallet onto the ground.

"See, it's this way, Major. You've got one woman who's used to—"

"Yeah, I see. Don't need an explanation."

Billy plunked his wiry body onto the bedroll he'd created by stitching two sheepskins together outside-in. "Like havin' two women in the same kitchen, don'tcha reckon? One cooks the eggs sunny-side, t'other mixes 'em up with a fork."

"Go to sleep." John snapped out the words like a command.

"Same thing with the—"

"Now!" The major shucked his boots and shrugged out of his buckskin shirt.

"—toast," Billy continued. "One'll want it so crisp it like to shatter your teeth, the other'll under-bake it so it balls up like warm dough in your mouth. Now myself, I prefer…you listenin', John?"

"Nope."

"Oh, well, in that case." Billy let three heartbeats go by. "Women are like that, too. Some are kinda stiff and they crumble easy. Others can take the heat. I like the kind that…Major?"

Silence.

"Aw, hell. And I was just gettin' to the interesting part."

Billy crawled into his sheepskin cocoon, gave John's motionless form a long, assessing look and then reached out and patted his shoulder. "Sleep good, Major. Ol' Billy here will protect you from sticker-weed and quicksand and renegade Indians.

"But I draw the line at pretty females. You're on your own, there."

More than an hour has passed and I am still shaking from the events of this evening. My hand flutters so I can scarcely guide the pen into the ink jar, and every line is blotted. What is the matter with me?

I do not normally muddle up over a fright, even one as unexpected as an encounter with an Indian (a starving Indian, from the look of him). Perhaps it is not that which has unnerved me.

Tonight the major spoke to me about Nettie. His words sent a cold knife right through me. Your sister bears watching. *At least I am assured I have not imagined Sister's unhelpful attitude. If I did not know better, I would judge her to be angry over something. Her mood at times seems almost sullen, and in her face I see more and more often that odd expression I began to note even before we left Liberty Corners, as if her mind is far, far away.*

Usually she relishes being at the center of every-thing. Never before have I seen her so…distant. Pre-occupied, *that is the only word I can come up with. I wonder but what she has left some young gentle-man behind, or perhaps she is pining still for Papa.*

I miss Papa so keenly at times I cannot draw breath. I long to sit down right then and bury my face in my apron and cry and cry. Nettie must feel even worse, as she was the center of his world. Poor lost Nettie. If no one loves her, she fancies she does not exist.

I love her, of course, despite her willful nature.

But for Nettie that is not enough.

It would surely be enough for me. But now that Papa is gone there is no one; I am all that she has left. I am all that I have left as well, for no one else in the world loves me, not even Nettie, deep down. I must care about myself since none other will.

I fear that is vain of me, but otherwise I shall shrivel inside like an old dry scrap of leather. If I allow that to happen, neither one of us will reach Oregon, as Papa had wanted.

My hand is steady now that I have written out my woes and heartache. My head nods toward the lan-tern.

Tomorrow I must talk to Nettie.

Chapter Eight

Constance turned the last of the butter she'd churned into a small square dish and pressed it down with a wooden paddle. "Nettie, take this over to Mrs. Ramsey, would you? And here…" She poured the remaining milky liquid into a jar. "This is for the baby."

Nettie eyed the container. "Oh, I do so love buttermilk. Couldn't we…?"

"Sister, that baby needs nourishment, more than that poor overworked woman can provide. You take it right on over this minute."

Nettie sent her a sulky look, and Constance bit her lower lip. She shouldn't have spoken so sharply. Reproaching her sister only made things worse: Nettie did not suffer even implied criticism with grace.

"I'll take it over," Nettie muttered, "but if I get invited to stay to their nooning, I will accept."

Constance lifted the dasher from the churn and dumped in a bucket of hot water. "You will do no such thing." She kept her voice gentle, but it was an effort. "Clara Ramsey has her hands full with six children and an almost empty larder. The last thing she needs is another mouth to feed."

"Cissy, you think too much. Don't you ever just do what feels good at the moment?"

Constance leveled a look at her sister. Nettie needed a stiff talking-to, but after driving the wagon since dawn and churning Molly's cream, she was too tired to broach even one of the difficulties she needed to sort out with her sister.

Oh, that is a run-away-and-hide excuse, and I know it. True, she was tired, her arms and shoulders stiff and achy from long hours keeping the oxen plodding forward. She'd dealt with Nettie's whims before, back in Liberty Corners when she'd spent the day boiling laundry or scrubbing floors. She didn't know why things were different now, but they were. Maybe it was crossing the land in a jouncing wagon and camping out on the endless, lonely plain every night. By day's end she was completely worn-out, her throat so parched that swallowing was an effort. She had no strength left to talk—argue more often than not—with her sister.

Another run-and-hide excuse. She scoured the inside of the churn with a boar bristle brush. The truth was, Nettie had changed. Right before her eyes, Nettie was growing prettier. And more self-absorbed.

"Just take the milk and butter to Clara," Constance said in a weary voice. "I haven't the energy to argue with you. And no," she added, "I do not do what 'feels good at the moment.' If I did, we would both starve."

Nettie grabbed up the dish of butter and the milk jar and flounced away across the camp toward the Ramsey wagon while Constance scrubbed the brush up and down the side of the wooden dasher. *If she stays for a meal with that struggling family I will...I will...*

What? Nettie was too big now to physically discipline, and words rolled off her like so many raindrops. "Besides," she muttered, "I'm not her mother anymore. I am her sister. We should be partners. Or at least friends." She forced back the tears that stung under her lids.

That was what she needed more than anything— a friend.

An empty feeling yawned in her belly. *God in heaven, I feel so alone.*

She clattered the lid on the churn and started for the back of the wagon. She'd just stow it and then cobble up some dinner. Beans again. Biscuits and beans. Corn bread and beans. Cold beans. Hot beans. Nettie was beginning to turn quite green at the sight of them.

Well, it couldn't be helped. It was all they had left until they reached Fort Kearny.

"Sufferin' fireflies, what're you doing with that old relic?"

Constance turned to see Billy West sitting on his paint-splashed pony, regarding her with snapping blue eyes.

"Churning butter. That 'old relic' is the best butter churn in Liberty Corners. My father made it."

"Sakes alive, woman, that's the plumb stupidest thing I ever seed you do. Jes' pour yer cream into a jar and tie it on the side of the wagon. Come suppertime, you'll have a hunk of butter big as a loaf of bread."

Billy's words brought her up short. Yes, she guessed it was stupid to labor over something that could be accomplished with little effort. Despite his forwardness, Constance paid attention to the man's advice. Billy West was trail-smart and intelligent. Besides, she rather liked his straight-talking manner. In fact, she relished the outspoken army man's company. When Mr. West came to supper, a sense of well-being filled her.

When it was Major Montgomery's turn to eat with

them, her body turned to mush and her mind sizzled with tension. She felt clumsy and slow, and usually she managed to spill something on him. Last night it was a whole platter of corn bread.

"Thank you, Billy. I will try out your butter-jar idea."

"Oh, ain't my idea, ma'am. 'Twas my superior officer taught it to me."

"Well, thank you anyway." His superior? Could he mean Major Montgomery? *The major could churn butter?*

"Miss Nettie around?"

"She took some of my butter over to Clara Ramsey."

"Then I'll stay a mite longer, that is if you don't mind."

"Not at all. Would you care to noon with us?" *How on earth had Major Montgomery learned to churn butter?*

"Oh, no, ma'am. The major'd have my hide mounted on a drying rack if I enjoyed myself much before sundown."

Constance stared at him. "Why is that, Billy?"

"Well, truth is, the major don't have much taste for the finer things of life. He'd rather bust his—uh, behind in the saddle eatin' hardtack and jerky than gettin' a whiff of perfume now and again. We had a big argument 'bout it last night.''

Perfume? She could just imagine whose. She turned to the shallow fire pit she'd dug and filled with buffalo chips. ''I'm just making corn bread and…'' She couldn't bring herself to say the word.

''Corn bread's good.'' Billy nodded with enthusiasm. ''Got any jam?''

''I'm afraid not.'' The last jar of strawberry preserves she'd put up the summer before had been eaten two nights ago.

''Got any molasses?''

''A little, yes.''

''I'd fergit the beans, then. Spread a bit of molasses over the top and it'll remind you of beans and fill you up just the same, but without the…just the same.''

''Did the major come up with this idea also?''

A puzzled look crossed Billy's clean-shaven face. ''Heck, no. The major don't like molasses. He likes his food 'straight,' if you take my meaning.''

''Straight?''

Billy leaned toward her. ''You know, Miss Constance,'' he said, his tone confidential. ''The major ain't like other men. Nothin' on his bread. Nothin' in his coffee. Nothin' fancy in his conversation. Just…straight.''

The word sent a shiver into her belly. Did he like his women "straight" as well?

Billy touched his hat. "Afternoon, Miss Constance. You tell Miss Nettie I stopped by. I'll be back around supper time—it's my turn tonight."

"You're always welcome, Billy."

He clicked his tongue at the pony. "I'll see if I can rustle up some coffee beans. That da—durn fool Duquette left half a sack settin' by the trail. Said it was moldy, but one time in the winter, John 'n me..."

He trotted off, still talking. Constance gazed after him until he reached the lead wagon where Joshua Duquette paced back and forth. She knew the man was in a frenzy to get rolling again. Nettie had told her Duquette and the major had had words. Duquette wanted to skip the noon rest stop; the major had prevailed with superior logic. With a midday break to eat and rest the oxen, they could travel another eight miles before dark. "Mr. Duquette was so mad he was shaking," Nettie had reported. "The major just stared him down. Oh, Cissy, it was thrilling!"

All at once she wasn't hungry for corn bread or molasses or anything else. She had to think what to cook for tomorrow's supper, when the major would join them.

No butter on his corn bread, hah! Well, then, she'd make a pie. Out of…something or other.

In the meantime she would decide what to say to Nettie when she returned. It was plain as the sun-burned nose on her face that her sister had disobeyed and stayed to eat with the Ramseys after all. *Oh, that girl.* Constance was responsible for her sister, but at times like these she no longer understood her.

As soon as she could slip away after supper, Constance left Nettie and Billy West to wash up the dishes and walked out onto the darkened prairie. The night seemed blacker, more impenetrable than before, but perhaps it was just her fear of the unknown.

She stumbled over a clump of dandelions and was suddenly aware of how much noise she was making. An Indian could find her with his eyes closed.

She raised her head and sucked in a breath. A figure stood some distance away. A man. Hatless, so she couldn't tell who—or what—he was.

Her heart began to pound. She pressed one hand to her chest, then glanced down at her feet. If she lifted her boots very, very carefully, she could walk back to the wagons in silence.

At the first step her toe scraped against a rock.

The man did not move, but stood looking up, his head tipped back in a way that was familiar.

Major Montgomery. Oh, thank the Lord. She wouldn't disturb him. He knew she was there. She could tell by the sudden stiffening of his shoulders.

What was he doing out here, just staring at the sky?

In a heartbeat, she knew. Her chest felt as if an ox had stepped on it.

Quietly she approached him and stood to his right.

He said nothing, just glanced at her and then looked back at the sky.

Without conscious effort, her lips opened. "You must have loved her very much." She spoke the words in a murmur, not expecting an answer.

He bowed his head.

She stood beside him in silence for minute after minute. They did not speak. After a while, close to a quarter of an hour, she guessed, they turned back toward the wagons at the same moment.

She took two steps and tripped over a patch of weeds. He slipped his hand under her elbow. The warmth of his hand on her bare skin sent a shiver all the way up to her scalp.

He had loved someone. The thought careened through her mind as she walked beside him, and all at once tears burned her eyes. A man and a woman who loved each other shut the rest of the world out.

Even when they were no longer together, they still belonged to each other in some way.

She wanted that. She wanted to love a man. To belong to him in that way. To give herself.

Oh, Lord, what was she thinking? Not this man. He loves another, and even though they are no longer together, he still belongs to her.

Pain ripped through her chest like a shard of hot iron. *I will not let it matter.* She could love whom she pleased. He did not have to love her in return.

She loved Nettie, but her sister did not really love her. Nettie merely needed her. And she loved this tall, silent man beside her.

The jolt of truth made her breath hiss in through her teeth. The major sent her an inquiring look, his eyes midnight-dark, his mouth opening to speak.

Constance shook her head.

And nearly tripped over a hillock of chickweed when he slipped his fingers from her elbow and took her hand.

Chapter Nine

The morning air lay hot and still over the camp. Nothing moved. No birds sang. Not one breath of wind stirred the elm leaves over her head. Despite the heat, Constance shivered on the wagon bench.

Far ahead she heard Mr. Duquette's gutteral shout, and one by one the wagons rolled forward. She craned her neck to see if her bread still rested in the crotch of the tree. On a day this stifling, the loaf would be bone-dry in an hour, even with the damp tea towel she'd wrapped it in. Still, she felt good about the gesture. No man, Indian or white, deserved to starve.

The Nylands' wagon ahead of her jerked and moved forward. She lifted the whip; their turn was next.

Nettie rode inside the wagon. Yesterday she had

fainted in the heat, and now she lay stretched out on her thin mattress while the young Ramsey girls sat beside her, waving a damp cloth over her head. Constance could hear their voices, like water murmuring over small stones. It sounded like music.

She closed her eyes, imagined Mama smoothing her hair and telling her stories or reading from the poetry book on a summer night. The sound of women's voices was the most beautiful sound in the world.

She and Nettie used to talk together like that. For the past day and a half, however, they had not spoken one word to each other. She opened her eyes and stared at the blurred grasslands.

Two hours passed. Three. Then four. There would be no nooning until they had crossed to the north side of the Platte River. Major Montgomery and Billy had selected the fording place, just east of O'Fallon's Bluff.

The undertaking filled her with dread. For miles and miles the river meandered lazily beside them, widening into shallow marshlands, then narrowing into confused freshets crisscrossed by sandbars. The water was too shallow for a ferry, too boggy to keep the overloaded wagons from sinking. Quicksand, Billy West had hinted.

Constance clamped her teeth together and

squinted into the sun. How would their oxen manage if the river was deeper than it looked? Could oxen swim when collared to a load?

The wagon train was strung out along the bank, eleven cumbersome, top-heavy wooden structures with sun-bleached canvas bonnets. They looked so small, so insignificant compared to the river. Like the stars in the dark heavens at night.

The sky turned yellow. A sudden breeze skittered the leaves of the elm trees, and then the wind picked up, bending the long grass into rippling gray-green waves. Constance pulled the oxen to a halt.

Every nerve in her body prickled. It was too quiet. Something was about to happen, she could feel it in her bones. On impulse, she set the brake and climbed down from the bench. She knew Nettie was safe in the wagon, but something about the day felt wrong.

Joshua Duquette barreled toward her, his boots scuffing up black dust. "What're you stopping for?" he yelled. "Get your damn wagon moving!"

Constance stared at him, but her mind was not on the wagon master. It was the utter silence that drew her attention. *That* was what was different—the silence.

"Listen," she said.

"Listen, hell. Get your wagon rolling before I—"

She raised one hand. "Listen," she insisted.

"There's nuthin' to hear, missy."

"Exactly," she said.

Duquette opened his mouth, then snapped it shut as the major rode up. "Circle the wagons," he shouted.

"What the hell for?" the wagon master shot back.

"Just do it. And do it now!"

Duquette spit off to one side. "Over my dead bod—"

"Suit yourself, Duquette. Constance, round up the Ramsey children. Quick."

She didn't question the order, just picked up her skirt and ran toward the three boys playing Keep-away with a dried buffalo chip. "Parker. Elijah. Jamie. Get to your wagon. Hurry."

Three blank white faces stared up at her.

"Hurry! Run as fast as you can!" She scooped up the youngest, Jamie, and raced across the flattening grass.

"Whatsa matter, Miss Constance?" Jamie cried. "Is it woofs or Injuns?"

"I don't know." She gasped out the words. "Just do what the major says."

Her breath hitched. Jamie whimpered and wound his arms around her neck, and she kept running.

By the time she'd hefted all three boys into the

back of their wagon and the waiting arms of Clara Ramsey, she could scarcely breathe. Her chest heaving, she stood while the other ten wagons pulled into a ragged circle around her Conestoga. Nettie will love being at the center, she thought irrationally.

All at once she felt entirely alone. Nettie was safe, the children were safe. She alone was responsible for herself.

She spotted the major driving the Ollesens' horses into a hastily rigged rope corral inside the wagon circle. Merciful heaven, the cow! She'd forgotten all about Molly. The speckled Jersey stood fifty yards beyond the wagons, placidly chewing her cud in the shade of a sycamore tree.

Constance started toward her. The sky darkened as if a kettle lid had been slapped over the sun. The wind tore at her skirt with such force she could scarcely take two steps in succession. She heard a shout and looked up to see the major's horse thundering toward her. He dismounted before the animal skidded to a stop and began to shout at her.

She couldn't understand what he was saying and shook her head.

His voice finally came to her, a single word floating on the wind. "Constance."

"What is it?" she screamed. "What is happening?"

He ran toward her, still shouting. "Dust storm."

By now the wind whined across the prairie like a hurt animal.

"My cow," she yelled. "Got to get Molly."

"No." He grabbed her upper arm. "Come with me."

They fought their way toward his mare, the wind snapping her skirt into his legs, tearing the breath from her mouth. She struggled to keep her eyes open.

The sky turned to clay and she looked up. A huge black ball rolled in front of the sun and kept coming toward them.

She felt his arm around her shoulder. "Get to the horse," he yelled.

"I can't see." She tried to make him hear, but he tipped his head into the wind and half pushed, half dragged her forward. She closed her eyes and let him guide her.

She could smell the mare. He scrabbled for something, then pulled a blanket over her head. "It'll be all right," he said into her ear. "Just face into the horse."

He pushed her forehead against the mare's warm neck.

Then, his arms braced on either side of her, he stepped in close. "Breathe through your mouth."

The wind howled, ripping at the covering that sheltered them. The horse stood still, but her breaths grew gusty and labored.

"She's choking," Constance said. "Cover her nose."

"Already did."

Under the quilt the air grew thick and gritty. She tasted dust on her tongue. And salt.

"Nettie?" she gasped.

"Billy's with her."

His low, calm voice made her light-headed with relief.

She would live through this. She would keep her mouth open, as he said. She would draw air in and out and she would survive. Nettie would survive. Her sister would be terrified, but Mr. West would be there.

At her back she felt the warmth of the major's hard body pressed against hers, felt his arms touching her hair.

"How long?" she managed to ask.

"Sometimes four, five hours."

"I can't..."

"Yes, you can. Don't think. Just keep breathing."

Obviously the major had experienced dust storms before. But he could not begin to imagine how frightened she was. It was as if the earth itself was shaking its feathers to rid itself of the flotsam that clung to its skin.

The wind dropped to a moan, then a whisper, and then was suddenly still. Neither of them moved.

She strained her ears, listening. All she could hear was the unsteady rasping of the man who imprisoned her. And at that exact moment the only thing she was conscious of feeling was his heartbeat thumping steadily against her spine.

Dear Lord, the man was holding her in his arms. Protecting her.

A hiccupy sob broke from her throat. How wonderful, how comforting it was to be held by a man, to feel his body hard and warm against hers. His forearms grazed her cheeks. For the first time in her life she acknowledged the ache of hunger for physical connection with another human being. If she moved a fraction of an inch in any direction she would touch this man's body.

How *could* she be so wanton!

Easily, she decided. Oh, so easily. The scent of his breath, his skin, the pungent spice-and-sweat smell of his clothes, his body, made her insides flutter. She heard him murmur a word at her back.

"Constance."

"Yes?"

A long, long silence.

"Don't—" He cleared his throat. "—don't move just yet. Don't turn around."

"Yes," she whispered. The last thing she wanted to do was break the spell that bound them. She waited.

"Oh, hell," he muttered at last. He turned her into his arms and bent his head.

She forgot about the dust and grit in her hair, about the wind, the horse. Even her sister seemed far away. She thought only of his mouth, the coffee and salt taste of his lips and tongue, the sharp, sweet jolt of pleasure that flared in her belly.

"Damn," she heard him whisper. And then he kissed her again, slower. Deeper.

In that moment, she knew nothing would ever be the same again.

Seven hours later, the wagons creaked into their last campsite before crossing the Platte. Nettie insisted on taking a bath. Constance brushed and brushed at the sand peppering Molly's hide. And after a supper of fried rabbit, which Billy West had snared and insisted on cooking with his "granddaddy's special sauce" of whiskey and chili peppers and the last of the molasses, Constance crawled into her pallet underneath the wagon.

She could not erase the memory of the major's

firm, warm lips on hers, or control the erratic rhythm of her heart when she remembered how she had felt just then—as if a steam engine had scooped her up onto the cowcatcher and was now climbing up, up to the top of the hill, toward…toward…

She could not even name it. She just knew that it was there, just over the horizon, waiting for her. She stared up at the underbelly of the wagon, thinking not of Nettie, as she usually did, but of the major.

And when she awoke the next morning, an even more startling surprise awaited her.

Chapter Ten

"Major! Major, wake up."

With an effort, John roused himself to a half-waking state. "What's wrong?"

"You was havin' another one of your dreams." Billy settled himself back on his sheepskin and closed his eyes.

"Sorry."

"Makes no matter, John. Jus' didn't want you to get to the screamin' part. Might get yourself shot by some nervous Nellie wagon master with more gun than he kin handle."

"Wasn't that kind of dream," John said. He had dreamed he was eating blackberries, so sweet they made his teeth ache. He drew in a long breath and realized he was hard.

What the—? He hadn't wakened up hard since...

He sucked in another lungful of air and smelled the rich scent of vanilla.

His quilt. He'd used it to cover Constance when the dust storm hit; the fabric still smelled like her.

He closed his eyes and concentrated on Billy's rattly snores. *You've lain awake before with an ache inside, John.* Yeah, he sure had. A thousand nights he'd listened to Billy's breathing. Tonight was the first time it didn't bother him.

Something had happened to him today. Out of a summer prairie dust storm, a black wind, the Cheyenne called it, something had been conceived as sure as a rutting buck covers a doe.

He knew it was his body talking, and it made him feel good. He wasn't dead after all. He was alive. The Indians would say "quick as Coyote," the clever spirit who cheated death. He was back among the living as Colonel Butterworth would put it, and he was damn glad.

He glanced down at the quilt, tented now over his male member, and chuckled. He was a man again. It was a good thing to know, even if he wasn't going to act on it.

He was also damn scared. He'd had enough of being a man to last two lifetimes.

Constance bent over the washboard doing her best to scrub the grass stains out of Cal Ollesen's trousers. The washtub, set over the fire beside her, blooped and sputtered as the men's shirts and underdrawers boiled. Nettie poked them with a hickory stick, but she kept her face averted. The lye soap smell nauseated her.

"I can't stir any longer, Cissy. I'm going to be..."

She dropped the stick and stumbled toward the wagon. Billy West took her place.

He gazed after Nettie, then turned his attention to Constance. "You know she's carrying, don'tcha?"

Constance raised her head but kept scrubbing. "Carrying what?"

Billy's smoke-colored eyebrows waggled. "Lordy, woman, you mean you don't know?"

"Don't know what? Billy, what *are* you talking about?"

"'Bout Miss Nettie, o' course. Like I said, she's carrying." He paused significantly. "You know, *carrying*." Another pause, then, "A babe."

Constance dropped the garment she was drubbing on the tin-ridged board, sending a splash of hot water over her apron. She scarcely noticed.

"A babe? Carrying a...you mean a baby?"

"She's pregnant, Miss Constance. I wasn't sure you knowed."

She put her reddened, soapy hand to her face.

Pregnant? Nettie was pregnant? She gripped the washboard for support. "No. Oh, no. *No.*"

"'Fraid so. 'Bout three months along, I'd say offhand."

She groaned aloud. It wasn't possible. In her wildest nightmares she had never imagined...

But it explained so much. Nettie's fatigue. Her headaches. Her moods and the crying. And lately, losing her breakfast most mornings. That was why Papa had insisted...

Her knees buckled. Papa had known. Oh God, Papa had known. Papa had tried to save Nettie's reputation by packing up and moving west, where people didn't know them.

"Billy, what are we going to do?"

"Damned if I know, Miss Constance. Jus' thought you oughtta see how things was." He stepped toward her, lifted her limp hand and placed it on the hickory stick.

"You stir 'em, honey. Ol' Billy'll scrub till you quit cryin'."

Today we crossed the Platte River. The sun was boiling hot over our heads, and the river a mile wide. It took three hours. To make it easier on the oxen, Arvo and Cal doubled the team and Nettie and

I walked. Well, waded, really. In we sloshed, shoes and all, for the water was so muddy I could not see bottom, and did not trust my bare feet to rocks or quicksand. It took forever to splash our way across.

Nettie and I have not spoken a single word all day long. She does not yet know that I am aware of her condition, but neither of us was inclined to converse as it took all our energy to hold our skirts above the water and keep walking.

My spirits are very low tonight. All day my throat ached with sadness, and my heart felt heavier than an old, worn wagon wheel. Whatever are we to do?

Of course, I must protect Nettie at all costs, but at times today I wanted to shake her until her teeth rattled.

I know that anger will not help matters. I must be of help and comfort, and I must think what to do. But, oh, the aggravation of it!

Billy West rode by once this evening, but he did not stop. I have not seen Major Montgomery since early morning, but I could not bring myself to walk out to view the stars with him after supper. I would be unable to hide my grief, and I cannot yet face the questions he would ask.

My sadness is like a gray pall thrown over my spirits. It pulls at me with insistent fingers, pokes hard at the places that hurt the most. Poor, poor Nettie. How lost and alone she must feel.

Constance faced her sister across the blanket they had spread near the fire after supper. "Nettie, we must talk."

Her sister looked up from the straw doll she was fashioning for Essie Ramsey. "Why must we?"

Her face wore the guileless expression Constance had come to recognize over the years. It was Nettie's protective veil. She dropped it between them whenever she had something to hide.

Constance tamped down her unease. She had to say something, but what? She couldn't stand the gulf between them any longer.

"An entire day and a half has passed and we have not exchanged so much as a good-morning."

"Well, then, good morning." Nettie ducked her head and worked away at the straw. Beside her, Essie and her twin sister sat watching with adoring eyes.

How she enchants them, Constance thought. *She is gifted in that way.* In many ways. Torn between love for her sister and fury at her duplicity, Constance worked to keep her voice even.

"It's no longer morning, Sister. It's getting dark. Ruth and Essie should be in bed."

"Ruth and Essie are staying with me tonight. I—you know how frightened I get at night. I thought some company would help."

Constance bit her lip. "I thought you liked your privacy, Sister. Would you like me to sleep in the wagon?"

"N-no, not really. I do like privacy. It's just that, well, the Ramsey wagon is so crowded...."

She was lying, Constance realized. Her sister didn't want to be near her. *And that is because she thinks she has something to hide from me.*

Well, she did, up until two days ago. But now that Constance knew her sister's secret, she was prepared to help bear the burden. Surely it would help Nettie to know that?

"The girls can climb into bed now, Nettie. I need to talk to you."

Nettie gathered up the doll makings and rose to her feet. "Ruth, Essie, time for bed. If you hurry, maybe there will be time for a story."

The twins raced to the wagon and clattered inside, their silvery voices floating out into the night. "A story! A l-o-n-g story!"

"'Bout a bear."

"No, 'bout a princess!"

Constance moved closer to Nettie. "You like children, don't you, pet?"

Nettie regarded her for a long minute. "You know, don't you, Cissy?" she said quietly.

"Yes, I know. Billy West told me."

Nettie's blue eyes widened. "Billy! I've told no one, especially that meddlesome old—how does *he* know?"

Constance took her sister's small, soft hand in hers. "He could see the change in you," she said gently. "I didn't see it, but Billy...well, I guess he's had experience in these matters."

"Oh, Cissy, I'm glad you know. It's been so hard keeping it inside. Sometimes I thought I would burst with needing to tell someone."

Constance stroked the back of her hand. "Did Papa know?"

"Yes. That's why he—Cissy, I am so ashamed. I've gone and ruined the entire family."

"Nonsense." Constance spoke with deliberate calm. "None of the family are left but for you and me. We will face this together."

Nettie began to sob. "Whatever shall I do?"

"Have you told the child's father?"

Her sister's head drooped. "Yes," she whispered. "But he cannot marry me."

"Why not?"

"It's Mr. Vickery, the vice president of Papa's

bank." She dabbed at her cheeks with the hem of her skirt. "He's already got a wife. And a third child on the way."

Constance nodded. "Bernard Vickery. I should have guessed."

"It was my fault, Cissy. I...flirted with him, led him on and...well, it was shameless of me, but I couldn't stand that he had a wife and it wasn't me. I've been sweet on him ever since I turned fourteen."

Constance stared at her sister. "So you told Papa, and Papa tried to save you by moving out west." She choked down the sick feeling in her heart. Papa had always given Nettie everything she'd ever wanted. This time, it had cost him his life.

"Cissy, you don't hate me, do you?"

Constance opened her mouth to answer, then closed it. She must be honest. She must be wise, as well. She was the only family Nettie had, now. She was mother, father *and* sister.

"I am angry, Nettie. I won't deny it. I am hurt and terribly upset, and just now I feel like screaming. But I do not hate you. You are my sister."

"Cissy, I am so scared."

"So am I, pet. I just wonder what we'll tell our grandchildren about *this*."

"I'll think of something," Nettie whispered. "I just know it will work out some way."

"Of course it will. Things have a way of sorting themselves out, one way or the other. For 'better or worse,' as they say."

"Yes," Nettie murmured.

Suddenly she stood up. "Good night, Cissy. I am glad we had this talk. I feel *so* much better!"

Constance watched her move to the wagon, her steps light and quick. She marveled at her sister's youthful resilience. Even bearing the heavy burden that she did, her motions were sure, her carriage full of energy. Why, she was practically skipping!

Chapter Eleven

In the baking heat of midafternoon, eleven wagons rumbled through the gate at Fort Kearny and creaked to a halt on the cottonwood-bordered parade ground. Major Montgomery dismounted and headed for the colonel's office.

"John!" Colonel Butterworth met him in the open doorway. "You're looking fit. Better than last time I saw you." He clapped the major's shoulder, then stood back to acknowledge the salute John mustered.

"Colonel," John acknowledged.

"How's the Duquette party managing?"

"They're hungry. And tired. Dust storm a day ago took all the starch out of them."

"Sutler's coming in tomorrow with a wagon load of supplies. You'll lay over a few days, of course."

"Wagon master's anxious to restock the food supplies and keep rolling."

"I'll talk to him." The colonel waved his arm at the big blue Conestoga. "That his rig?"

"Nope. That's the Weldon sisters' wagon."

Colonel Butterworth shot him a look. "Sisters, eh? Old or young?"

John ignored the question. "Come on, I'll introduce you to Joshua Duquette."

"'Druther meet the sisters," the older man said with a wink. "Either of them pretty?"

"Harry, you want me to tell Martha you're turning mooney over a spinster and her kid sister?"

"Not pretty, eh?"

"Didn't say that," John replied. "Anyway, judge for yourself, they're coming this way."

The colonel stepped off the porch. "That Duquette behind them?"

John hid a grin. "Something wrong with your eyesight, Harry? That's Billy West."

The colonel stopped short and narrowed his gaze. "Nothing wrong with it, just don't believe what I'm seeing." He shook his head in disbelief. "Billy West without a beard. What's the cavalry coming to?"

"It's going straight to hell, Colonel. He even took a bath in the river last night."

"And the ladies?" the older man intoned to John beside him as they moved forward.

"Miss Constance Weldon, Miss Henrietta Weldon, may I present Colonel Butterworth?"

Nettie made a little twittering sound and started to curtsy, then changed her mind and extended her hand, little finger crooked. "I am utterly charmed, Colonel."

"The pleasure is mine, I assure you." He bowed over her fingers.

Constance stepped forward. "I have extra butter and cream today from our cow. Would you or your officers care for some?"

"Well, now." The colonel's face shone with interest. "That is kind of you, Miss Weldon. Isn't often we get fresh cream out here." He acknowledged Billy with a nod, then returned his gaze to Constance.

"Supply train is due in tomorrow. I supposed you'd be low on food, so the officers invite you to mess with them this evening. Later, Mrs. Butterworth requests some dancing, that is if we can find a fiddler somewhere." He sent a questioning look at Billy.

Constance opened her mouth to reply, then heard Nettie's voice at her side. "Why, how perfectly wonderful! A dance! I've always loved military balls. They are so terribly elegant, don't you think?''

''Nettie, for goodness' sakes.'' She was appalled at her sister's airs. Where had she learned such nonsense?

''It's not a 'ball,' my dear,'' the colonel said kindly. ''Out here things are pretty rough-and-tumble. A room full of my officers stomping out a two-step is a long way from 'elegant.'''

Nettie's eyes sparkled. ''Oh, Colonel Butterworth, I am quite sure you are exaggerating just to tease me.''

Constance met John's gaze, and when he rolled his eyes she nearly laughed out loud. The corners of his mouth twitched. Well, it *was* funny. Ridiculous, even. She dropped her head and studied her shoe tops until she could control her voice.

''Nettie, come help me with the milking.''

''Now? You don't usually milk until supper—''

''Now, Nettie. The colonel has other duties, I'm sure.''

John gestured behind them. ''There's Duquette now, Colonel. You wanted to meet him?''

The two men moved off, and after a moment, Billy West fell into step behind them. Constance couldn't help noticing how the major towered over Colonel Butterworth.

"Cissy, you're so mean sometimes. I wanted to engage in a bit of civilized conversation."

With a sigh, Constance turned her attention to Nettie. "Colonel Butterworth has an entire army post to look after. I would guess conversing with a very forward young woman is not one of his priorities."

Nettie stuck out her lower lip. "But he was ever so nice to me, didn't you think? Cissy? Why are you looking at me like that?"

"Dear Sister..." *How can I say this without being hurtful?* "You are so young and pretty and full of life sometimes you might not notice...things. Perhaps it is time you realized the world—the wagon train we travel with, the fort we take shelter in— these things do not revolve around you."

Nettie's chin came up. "Of course I realize that. You just don't want me to have any fun."

"Fun!" She stared at her sister. "Nettie, you are three months gone in the family way. You should be thinking of more serious matters." She laid her arm about Nettie's shoulders and turned her toward the wagons. "Here comes Cal to unhitch the oxen."

"Oh, pooh on Cal. All he ever does is look moony-eyes at me, and if I even say boo to him, he stammers. Why, he can't even read."

"What does reading have to do with a man's worth?"

"Cal Ollesen isn't a man," Nettie scoffed. "He's a boy."

"Cal is the same age you are. Seventeen."

"He's never going to amount to anything, Cissy. He and Arvo are, well, they're immigrants."

"So they may be, Nettie, but I think Cal and Arvo will prosper. They work hard. Their horses show good care."

"Oh, well, you know what I mean, Cissy."

Constance put her hands on her sister's shoulders. "And when it comes to being immigrants, Sister, what do you think *we* are? Granny Weldon came from Ireland as a bride. And Great-Aunt Flora on Mama's side sailed from England with her two babes in a basket and worked three years as a—"

Nettie's groan stopped her. "Not that again."

"I am sorry, pet. You are right, such talk is not what is needed at this time."

"It certainly isn't," Nettie snapped. "What I need," she said in an undertone, "is to talk to Colonel Butterworth. Or maybe the colonel's wife."

Constance hurried forward. "Cal." She waved at the lanky blond youth. "We are all invited to supper tonight and dancing afterward. Tell Arvo and the

Ramseys, will you? And I have your clean shirts ready in the wagon."

Cal bobbed his head and tried to keep his eyes off Nettie. "T'anks, Miss Constance. I unhitch your team now."

"Thank you, Cal. It—Nettie, where are you going?"

Nettie spun to face her. "I am going to pay a social call on the colonel's wife."

"But…"

"It's important, Cissy. Get Cal to help with the milking."

"Important? Whatever do you mean?"

"Don't try to stop me, Cissy. I know exactly what I'm doing." She turned on her heel and walked off.

Constance stared after her.

"She iss yust like my mare, Ilsa," Cal said. "Headstrong and…oh, so beautiful. So full of spirit."

Headstrong. Oh, my yes. Nettie was just like Mama. Just like Great-Aunt Flora. Neither one of them ever gave an inch, and in the end it killed them both.

A bolt of fear ripped through her belly, followed by a fierce surge of protectiveness. Nothing was going to happen to Nettie. *Nothing*. She would give her life for her sister.

* * *

"How do I look, Cissy?" Nettie spread the skirt of her green printed dimity and twirled around for effect.

Constance gazed on her sister's still-slim form. "You look like an angel, dearest. A beautiful angel with silver hair and lovely blue eyes."

"I packed this dress at the bottom of the trunk, and it took ever so long to dig it out. I found your yellow striped muslin, too, but I fear it needs pressing."

She didn't even remember bringing the dress Nettie spoke of. She'd worn the simply cut plain brown prairie dress and long muslin apron for so long it felt as if they were part of her. Except for an occasional washing, she'd scarcely been out of her clothes. Her underclothes she wore all day and slept in at night; by now, the garments could probably stand up by themselves.

She didn't feel clean enough to step into the yellow gown, but oh, how she longed to wear something pretty and not worry about the hem dragging in the mud or the sun burning her exposed neck and shoulders.

She lifted the sadiron from its niche next to the coffee mill and set it near the fire. Even half-heated it would press out the creases in the tiered skirt.

Nettie stepped back into the wagon and Constance

heard the song her sister always hummed when she brushed her hair. "Beautiful Dreamer." Unconsciously her hand went to the single dark braid down her back. Was there enough water to take a spit bath and wash her hair?

She peeked into the tin water bucket over the fire. Nettie had used two-thirds of it. She would have to make do with what was left.

Nettie reemerged, a black knitted shawl around her shoulders. "I'm going to help the colonel's wife set up the supper table," she announced.

"That is thoughtful of you, Sister. Take the crock of butter and the cream with you."

Twin spots of color rose on Nettie's cheeks. "I— I'm not going there directly," she said. "First I have to…have to stop by the Ramseys," she added quickly. "And…and tell Essie and Ruth their bedtime story. Isn't it dear of them to want it so? Mrs. Ramsey says they won't go to sleep at night without it, and she's too worn-out by evening."

Constance caught her sister's gaze and held it. "Take Mrs. Ramsey the other crock of butter, then," she said in an even tone.

"Oh, Cissy, do I have to? I'll get grease all over my dress."

"No butter crock of mine has a spot of grease on

the outside, pet. Not even your fingers will be soiled. Now, go.''

It wasn't what she'd wanted to say. She'd wanted to scream at Nettie, get her to stop shirking. She opened her mouth to call her back, but her sister had slipped around the corner of the wagon and disappeared. In a few moments Constance watched the slim figure in a swirling green skirt march toward the Ramsey wagon, a butter crock in each hand.

''She forgot the jug of cream for Mrs. Butterworth,'' she said under her breath.

Or maybe she left it behind on purpose. She remembered how Nettie could always wheedle sweets and grown-up privileges from Papa. From the time she was four years old, Nettie had done things her own way. Even now, she often sneaked an extra biscuit at supper, and just as often pleaded a headache to avoid the washing up.

But, Constance reminded herself, Nettie was carrying a child. She hadn't known that before; now that she did, she must remember to make allowances.

She hefted the bucket of warm water up into the wagon and climbed in after it, then scrubbed her sun-parched skin with a sliver of the scented soap she'd brought from home. Shivering, she unwound her braid and brushed her hair thoroughly using an extra cup of water she'd saved.

When the sadiron was heated, she spread the yellow muslin on Nettie's pallet and began smoothing out the wrinkles. She'd accomplished the task a thousand times in the kitchen back home, but working on her knees with a half-heated iron was exhausting. By the time she finished, her wrist ached and her back was stiff.

Why are you going to all this trouble? a voice teased. Nettie is the pretty one. She'll have half the officers eating out of her hand before supper, and the other half after dessert.

She loved seeing her sister at social gatherings. Nettie was happiest surrounded by admirers. Even the women fussed and cooed over her. Later they would compliment Constance on what a good job she'd done raising her younger sister.

Tonight for some reason, Constance wanted to be pretty, too. She wanted to enjoy herself, wanted to lose herself in the fiddle music and dance until the stars came out. Nettie had chafed under the discipline of their dancing lessons back home, but Constance loved the intricate steps of the Carolina Quadrille and schottisches and waltzes that dipped and looped about the floor. With a start she realized she hadn't been to a dance since…

Since last Fourth of July. Almost a year ago. She

was a different person now. Older. More frightened of what lay ahead now that she'd experienced some of it. But more sure than ever that she was doing the right thing.

The yellow muslin settled over her head, and she buttoned up the bodice with trembling fingers. The sleeves stopped at the elbows with a ribbon tie and a flare of lace. Her exposed forearms were brown as berries from the sun, and her neck…she craned her head toward the mirror on Mama's dresser. From her chest to her ears the skin was sun-bronzed and the freckles across her nose were more numerous than ever.

She sighed. How *did* Nettie keep her skin so white?

By walking on the shady side with the children while you drive the wagon straight into the sun all day. Besides Nettie wears a broad-brimmed hat and never rolls up her sleeves.

And so should she, herself. It was high time she took some care with her own appearance. The major would think she had no graces whatever.

Her chest gave a funny little squeeze. She stepped down from the wagon and gazed across the parade ground, now ringed with wagons. A flag snapped on a pole in the center of the square. She gazed beyond it to the row of five unpainted houses that served as officers' quarters.

Which one did the major occupy? The large two-story one with the wide porch across the front? Probably that was Colonel and Mrs. Butterworth's.

Oh, the cream! Quickly she gathered her hair at her nape and tied it with a scrap of ribbon. Then she banked the fire, grabbed up the cream jug in one hand and her shawl in the other and set off for the officers' mess.

The collection of adobe buildings with sod roofs to the right must be the soldiers' barracks. First Nebraska Cavalry, the weathered sign on the first building read. The second, a two-story structure, had a painted sign that swung between two posts driven into the ground. Seventh Iowa Cavalry.

Which one was the major's unit? The Iowa Seventh, perhaps. His manners seemed more Eastern in a way. But he wore that buckskin shirt as if he'd been born in it, and he'd had contact with the Indians, so perhaps the First Nebraska? She would ask him tonight.

Her heart lurched at the thought of being close enough to speak to him for the first time in two days. He had kissed her! Not once, but twice.

At the time it felt like the most natural thing in the world, being in his arms, inhaling the scent of his clothes, his skin. His breath.

But now she wondered about it. Why *had* he kissed her? And held her like that?

And why, Lord help me, did I like it so much?

Chapter Twelve

Each step Constance took across the parade ground to the long, low adobe building that served as the officers' dining hall increased the fluttery feeling in her chest. Never before had she felt so nervous at the prospect of a social gathering. Or maybe it was Colonel Butterworth's mention of dancing afterward.

She'd been to dozens of dances and socials and tea parties in Liberty Corners. After a few minutes' conversation or a waltz or two, the young men who partnered her would drift off, leaving Constance to spend the evening on the sidelines talking with the chaperones. Here, in the middle of Nebraska Territory, would it be any different? Would she end up discussing the price of wool challis and remedies for fever sores with the older women while Nettie floated about the room on the arm of one partner after another?

Tonight, she resolved, if asked to dance she would not open her mouth except to smile at her partner. That was what men wanted—adoring looks and inane chatter.

The mess hall interior felt airy and cool after the heat on the parade ground. Two long tables were laid with spotless white cloths and speckled blue enamelware plates. Constance moved toward Martha Butterworth, who was arranging a bouquet of wild lupine at the end of one table, and presented the cream jug.

The plump woman in a rose cambric dress beamed. "Ah, bless you, my dear! The colonel hasn't had cream for his coffee since March." She set the jug down at the head of the table.

Constance extended her hand. "I am Constance Weldon. I believe my sister, Nettie, was to deliver a crock of butter?"

"Oh, yes." The colonel's wife squeezed her fingers. "I cannot thank you enough for your offerings, Miss Weldon. Nettie has been here and gone."

"Gone? Gone where?"

Mrs. Butterworth gave her hand another squeeze. "Now don't you concern yourself, dear. Your sister has gone for a walk about the compound with the colonel, and I must tell you she is without a doubt the sweetest, prettiest thing he's laid eyes on for ages. Why, the colonel's spirits were considerably raised by her visit this afternoon."

Constance searched the snapping blue eyes of the woman who imprisoned her hand. "Her visit? She mentioned she wished to pay her respects, but..."

"And so she did," Mrs. Butterworth chirped. "And then some. The colonel is simply delighted with her. He has been so worried about the major."

Constance jerked her head up. "The major?"

"Major Montgomery, my dear. Surely you know he's going on to Fort Laramie with you?"

"N-no, I did not know." The rush of joy she felt at the news evaporated as she puzzled over the connection.

"Why?" she said without thinking. "Why is Colonel Butterworth delighted?"

At that moment, the screen door banged open and the five Ramsey children tumbled in, followed by their parents, Enos and Clara Ramsey. Clara lugged her baby daughter on one hip. Behind them crowded the others—Cal and Arvo, the Nylands, old Mrs. Stryker, even Joshua Duquette, his boots polished and his hair slicked down.

Mrs. Butterworth patted her arm. "Forgive me, my dear. I must fly to my duties as hostess. Please make yourself at home.'' She gestured toward the flower-decorated table. ''It is the colonel's specific request that you dine with us.''

Her rose skirt swaying, the colonel's wife whisked away toward the growing crowd of travelers pouring through the doorway. While Constance stared after her, Nettie entered on the arm of a slim, red-haired officer with an elaborate handlebar mustache.

''Cissy, this is Lieutenant Thompson.''

The young man swiped off his cap. ''I'm honored, ma'am. I have instructions to seat you and Miss Nettie at the head table. If you'll follow me, ma'am.''

Nettie swept ahead on the lieutenant's arm and took the place he indicated, to the right of the colonel's chair. Constance seated herself across from her, wondering why Nettie refused to meet her gaze.

Essie and Ruth Ramsey tumbled over each other in their eagerness to get close to Nettie. She leaned down and said, ''You must sit with your family, girls. Run along, now.''

''Won't we have a story?'' Essie asked, her brown eyes filling.

''Not tonight.''

Ruth took her sister's hand. ''Tomorrow?''

''Yes, tomorrow. I promise. A long story,

about…about a boy that turns into a scaly green dragon.''

''Ohh,'' the sisters said in unison. Nettie turned them about and gave them a little push.

Colonel and Mrs. Butterworth made their way to the table and seated themselves. With a brisk nod, Martha Butterworth signaled that supper was to commence.

The next thing Constance knew every square inch of her plate was filled with broiled meat, mashed potatoes swimming in gravy, and green peas. She hadn't seen this much food since their last meal in Independence.

Lieutenant Thompson and six other officers in blue uniforms found places at the two tables, and as the cook's assistants moved among the diners filling plates, Constance searched for Major Montgomery.

He wasn't present. Instinctively she guessed the major disliked eating in a noisy, crowded room full of chatter and the clink of knives and forks. She'd bet he and Billy West were sharing a simpler supper, and maybe some whiskey, over a campfire.

Something in the way Nettie's head tilted toward the colonel, then toward the redheaded lieutenant to her right made Constance pause. She caught Mrs. Butterworth's eye at the other end of the table, and when the older woman flashed her a broad smile, Constance dipped her head in response.

All was well, was it not? Nettie was in her element, flanked as usual by admirers. Food was plentiful. They were warm and safe inside a building with four sturdy walls, but…what?

An undercurrent of unease prodded at the back of her mind.

She picked up her fork, ate two bites of mashed potatoes and set the utensil down. Her stomach closed in on itself. It was sinful to waste all that food, but she couldn't help it. She couldn't eat one more mouthful.

She watched Nettie gobble down forkful after forkful of meat and potatoes until her plate was almost empty. She sent Constance a quick, questioning look, and without a word, Constance handed over her plate. She wasn't hungry, and besides, Nettie was eating for two now.

When dessert came, Constance offered her dish of apple cobbler to her sister as well, and sipped her coffee in silence until Colonel Butterworth rose from his place, indicating that supper was over. Constance offered up a silent prayer of thanks. If she had to sit still one more minute, she'd pop.

"Dancing will commence in thirty minutes," the

colonel announced. "Gentlemen, apply yourself to clearing the floor."

Dancing! She had almost forgotten about it. She watched the officers and men of the wagon train shove tables and benches against the walls. Clara Ramsey gathered up her brood and herded them out the door to bed them down in their wagon. Old Mrs. Stryker volunteered to watch over them so Clara and Enos could return to the dancing.

Constance needed a breath of air before she faced the rest of the evening. She slipped out the screen door onto the long verandah and tipped her head up. The air smelled of grass and wood smoke. A huge gold moon hung low in the sky, and the darkness was soft and inviting.

She didn't feel like dancing. She felt like walking out into the night, gazing up at the stars. A whippoorwill called, and after a moment another answered. The sounds spoke of the connection between living things. Of belonging.

A wave of love and protectiveness for Nettie swept over her. They, too, were connected, not only by blood, but by the unshakable bond that linked them together. They were sisters. They had shared joys and sorrows, shared their growing up. They would share in each other's lives until the hour of death parted them.

Out of the smoky dark strode a familiar lanky figure.

"Cain't have dancin' 'less you got a fiddle," Billy West rasped. "And I guess I'm it. Leastways, that's what the colonel is suggestin'."

Constance stepped off the porch. "I didn't know you played the fiddle, Billy."

"To be truthful, there's some say I can't. But once my bow arm gets movin' it doesn't want to slow down, so I just hold the fiddle up to it and see what happens." He patted the instrument he carried under his arm. "What's yer favorite song, Miss Constance?"

"'Beautiful Dreamer.' My mother used to play it on the piano."

"Ol' Billy'll play it for you tonight."

Constance smiled at him. "Well, then," she quipped, "ol' Constance will waltz."

Billy cackled appreciatively. "You're not old, Miss Constance. It just seems that way cuz Miss Nettie's so young. You're all growed-up. Nettie, now, she's got a ways to go yet."

Constance stared at the sun-leathered face before her. What an odd sort of fellow Billy was. She liked him, though. He might poke his nose in other people's business, but he understood things. And he usually made good sense. She hadn't used the butter churn since he'd explained his Mason jar method; probably he was right about Nettie, too.

And about herself, as well.

But this particular evening she didn't feel "all growed-up." She felt unsure and off balance and...hungry for something that wasn't meat or mashed potatoes.

When Billy struck up the first notes of a reel on his fiddle, the entire mess hall transformed itself from a noisy throng into two long, orderly lines waiting expectantly for the grand march.

Outside the screen door, Major Montgomery watched the goings-on with halfhearted interest. He disliked the rare dances held at the post when a wagon train came through. He and Billy had shared a spitted rabbit and half a bottle of whiskey over a campfire on the other side of the compound. After supper, Billy had kicked the fire out early and grabbed his fiddle; John had decided he'd turn in and sleep off the drink, but now he found himself on the verandah, looking on unseen for want of anything better to do. At least that's what he told himself.

He shot a glance across the grounds at the unpainted two-story frame house where he was officially quartered. A young lieutenant, a bachelor, was supposed to have moved in just after John and Billy had ridden out to meet the wagon train. Hell, he didn't even know what the fellow looked like. If he wanted, he could have the whole place to himself until the dance broke up. Later, if the lieutenant talked too much, he'd camp out with Billy again. In the meantime, he'd just listen to Billy's fiddle.

The music rolled out of the instrument like sap from a sugar maple. The line of dancers swept toward each other, then back, and the first couple joined hands and sidestepped down the length of the hall. It was Nettie Weldon and a redheaded partner.

John watched them for a moment, and just as he turned away, his gaze settled on the second couple in line. A dress like yellow sunshine and a fall of dark, wavy hair past her shoulders. He didn't recognize her until she turned her face toward her partner.

Something inside him went completely still. Constance. His stomach tipped upside down. He could scarcely breathe she was so beautiful.

The fact that she was circling the room with Arvo Ollesen sent a blade of anger into his gut. He wanted no other man to lay his hand on her.

He watched until he couldn't stand it, then tramped off the porch toward his quarters. He reached the weathered front door before he came to his senses.

You want to dance with her? Hold her in your arms? What's stopping you?

Certainly not Arvo, or any other man. He reversed direction. He guessed he must be a little drunk. John Marshall Montgomery never did anything on impulse.

He could walk steadily enough, could see and hear just dandy, but his brain seemed a little…overheated. Not thinking too clearly.

Or was he? He'd thought of little but Constance Weldon and those clear, assessing eyes of hers since the first day he'd laid eyes on her. Truth was, he was thinking a lot clearer than he wanted. He was beginning to know things—about himself, about his feelings—things he wished he'd left buried.

He wanted *his* hands on her. His and nobody else's.

The realization brought him to a halt with one hand on the door latch. What right did he have?

"Ah, John, there you are," Colonel Butterworth grumbled from the other side of the screen. "Come on in here and join the dancing."

"Colonel," John acknowledged in a monotone. He ducked under the low door frame and straightened.

The colonel clapped him on the back. "Well done, Major. I'm proud of you." He eyed John's buckskin shirt. "Even if you are out of uniform."

John chuckled. "Neither Billy nor I spend much time *in* uniform, Colonel. You know that."

"Still, I would have thought for such an occasion...well, never mind that. Martha still thinks you're the best-looking officer at the post, no matter what you're wearing. Jehoshaphat, Major, what is it you *do* to women that gets them so het up?"

"Harry?"

The colonel turned a bland face on him. "Yes, John?"

"Mind your own business."

"To be sure, Major," Colonel Butterworth said with a laugh. "Any minute now. Well, don't stand there in the doorway waiting for an invitation, come on in."

The reel ended with a flourish of notes from Billy's fiddle. The colonel moved away, and John watched the older man join the spirited, pretty woman in rose sateen who was presiding over the refreshment table, slip an arm about her waist and say something in her ear.

Coffee seemed like a good idea. He headed across the room toward the big silver coffee urn.

"John!" The colonel's wife stood on tiptoe,

kissed his cheek, then kissed the other and then, in a rush of giggles, repeated the entire process. "You dear, darling man! How proud we all are of you."

"I've brought in wagon trains before, ma'am. What's so special about this one?"

"Modest as ever, I see," she burbled. "I must be off now to pour out, but we will talk tomorrow." She bustled back to her station at the coffee and punch table.

John shook his head at her retreating figure. Things were beginning to make no sense at all.

"Next dance'll be 'Strawberry Jam Polka'," Billy yelled.

John dodged the milling couples and accepted a mug of steaming black coffee from Martha Butterworth. Edging away from the table and her piercing blue eyes, he leaned against the whitewashed adobe wall and sipped the brew. "Strawberry Jam Polka" was Billy's favorite. John knew the tune by heart, since Billy hummed a good deal after supper, but even so he'd never had the least inclination to hop up and down in those particular steps. Waltzing was more his style. He wrapped both hands around his mug and wished he was outside looking at the stars.

A blur of yellow whirled past him, enclosed in the possessive grasp of Joshua Duquette. Without conscious thought, John replaced the unfinished mug of coffee on the table and moved forward.

He intercepted Duquette's path, stepped in and spun Constance out of the wagon master's arms and into his own.

"Hey, whaddya think you're doing?" Duquette's already florid color deepened.

At that instant, John's thoughts got mixed up with his tongue. He meant to utter a civilized, *Mind if I cut in?* What actually came out was, "Take your hands off her."

He left Duquette blinking in astonishment and whirled Constance away. At the edge of the crowd, she pulled him to a stop.

"Am I dreaming, or did you really say that? Tell him to take his...?"

Now he wasn't sure. Must be drunker than he thought. "Don't remember. Care to dance?" He moved closer, spread one hand across her back and pulled her into a waltz.

"I—I believe this is a polka, Major."

"I know." He kept on waltzing.

"Major? This music is in four-four time, not waltz time."

"I know that, too."

She drew in a breath, and her soft, lacy bodice

brushed his chest. He imagined the tips of her breasts touching him.

"I take it you do not like the polka, Major? I thought everybody out west liked the polka, and Billy is playing it so nicely, don't you think so? I had no idea he played the fiddle. It makes such a lovely sound."

She gulped air and rushed on. "Do you play an instrument, Major? Mama taught me to play the piano, and I tried to teach Nettie, but…do you like the piano, Major?"

He looked down into her face. "You going to stop talking sometime?"

Her cheeks went crimson. "Oh. I thought men preferred women to chatter."

"Some men might. This one doesn't."

"Oh," she said again. She caught her lower lip between her teeth. "I am sorry, Major."

"Stop calling me 'Major'," he said in a voice he didn't recognize. "Dammit, Constance, you know my given name."

"I do," she murmured.

"Then use it. We've been close enough to warrant it."

"I—"

She moved with him in silence, so light on her feet she seemed to float in concert with him, her body responsive to his every subtle move. And still they waltzed to the polka music.

Suddenly the music changed. The strains of "Beautiful Dreamer" rose, fitting their steps exactly. Constance smiled. "Billy said he would play that for me. It was my mother's favorite song."

"My mother's as well."

She looked up at him. "Not really?"

The scent of her skin made him light-headed. "Yes, really. Mother played the harp." He'd never before told anyone the smallest detail about his mother. Not even…

An overwhelming urge came over him to be closer to the woman in his arms. He tightened the hand at her back, pulled her toward him until his chin grazed her temple. Her hair smelled of flowers, roses maybe. Sweet and spicy at the same time.

And oh God, she was warm and alive against him. He closed his eyes.

"John?" came a low whisper.

"Yes?"

"Where did you grow up?"

"Philadelphia." He spoke the word into her hair, let his lips rest there for a moment.

"Constance?"

A slight hesitation. "Yes?"

"Don't talk," he murmured. "Just dance. Just…be here with me."

Chapter Thirteen

He wanted to kiss her so bad his arms trembled. Maybe it would be better if she *did* talk.

But she didn't. She moved with him as if she could read his body, her skirt tangling between his knees, one hand clasped in his, the other resting on his shoulder. Through the buckskin her fingers burned into his skin.

He wanted it. All of it.

Her.

Lord God, he was falling in love with her.

He laughed out loud, and she tipped her head up, her eyes questioning.

"It's nothing," he lied. *It is everything.* "I am... surprised at something," he said when he could speak.

You're scared out of your skin.

"Oh? Surprised at what?" Her voice ran over him like clear water.

"That I'm here, at Fort Kearny. In the mess hall." He took a short breath between each admission. "Dancing. With you." Every word he spoke seemed unbelievable. A fortnight ago he'd lost interest in living. Now...

Now he felt his body throb with life. With hunger.

"There's more," he said against her temple. "That day I kissed you, remember? I didn't want to stop."

He felt a tremor go through her. "I remember," she said softly. "I didn't want you to stop."

Oh God. Oh God. A sweet ache dipped into his belly. "Constance," he breathed. "Constance, I—"

"Ladies and gentlemen?" The colonel was rapping a spoon against a coffee mug. "If I might have your attention?"

The fiddle squawked to a stop and in the silence a beaming Colonel Butterworth stepped forward. "I have an important announcement."

John turned Constance in his arms and stood at her back, facing the colonel. After a moment he pulled her against him so her spine pressed into his chest. He fought to keep just the one hand resting on her shoulder.

"Folks." Colonel Butterworth's voice rose. "I

take great pleasure in announcing an engagement tonight. One of our guests here this evening, Miss Nettie Weldon, is to marry soon.''

A buzz of voices, and then clapping. Constance went rigid.

John bent forward. "Did you know about this?" he whispered.

She shook her head. "I never know what Nettie's going to do."

Colonel Butterworth rapped the spoon for quiet. "Here's the best part, folks. Miss Nettie is going to marry none other than Major John Montgomery!"

John's fingers dug into Constance's shoulder. "What the devil?"

"That's not true!" he shouted. But his voice was lost amid cheers and stomping feet.

Constance turned to face him. She looked as if he had struck her.

"It's not true, Constance. It's a mistake, a misunderstanding. Surely you don't think—"

An awful moment stretched between them. Then she looked up at him and smiled. "No, John, I don't. It's Nettie's doing. I should have guessed."

"I'll go to the colonel and explain."

She stopped him with a look. "No. At least not yet. It would shame Nettie even more than—" She bit off her sentence.

"Even more than what?"

"Come outside, John. I will explain."

The screen door slapped shut behind them. John spoke first. He caught her shoulder and turned her to face him. "She's pregnant, isn't she?"

Constance swallowed. "It was Papa's banking associate. He's married."

All at once he was cold sober. "When will it be born?" John heard his voice snap out the question.

"Around Christmastime, I would guess."

"How did—?"

"It was Billy West who called it to my attention."

"That sharp-eyed son of a—"

"He was trying to help, John." Her voice shook just the tiniest bit.

He nodded. *God Almighty, where did this leave him and Constance?*

She licked her lips. "I think," she said carefully, "they are calling for you inside."

"Let them."

"Please, please, don't shame her, John. She is my sister. I cannot bear to see her hurt."

"I won't let her manipulate me into this."

"No, she must not. In the meantime…can we not undo the damage after we leave the fort?"

He was quiet for a long minute. "All right, I'll

play out her little charade tonight. Tomorrow I'm going to tan her backside.''

"You will do no such thing, John,'' Constance said gently. "She is carrying a child.''

"Damn,'' he muttered.

"Besides,'' she said. "Tomorrow I myself am going to give her a talking-to she'll never forget.''

Besieged by well-wishers, John fought his way across the dining hall to confront Colonel Butterworth. "What the hell's got into you, Harry?''

"My boy.'' The colonel set his punch cup down on a nearby table. "Seeing how circumstances stand, I thought I'd do you a favor by moving things along.''

"Moving *what* things along? Goddammit, Colonel—''

"Now, John. Miss Nettie and I had a long walk this afternoon, during which she told me all about it.''

"All about what?'' John clenched his hands at his back for fear he'd forget himself and thrash his commanding officer.

"About compromising her, John.'' The colonel stepped toward him and lowered his voice. "It's nothing to be ashamed of. I'm happy you've found someone.''

"I care nothing for Nettie Weldon," John said through gritted teeth. "Nothing!"

"Doesn't matter now, son. She's in the family way, and—"

"Well, I didn't get her there."

Colonel Butterworth went on as if he hadn't heard a word John uttered. "—and I expect an invitation to the wedding. There's a preacher at Fort Laramie. You can get married there."

"Like hell I will. Harry, you call this off. Call Nettie's bluff."

The colonel's face hardened. "You're going to marry that girl, John, and that's an order. Unless," he said, lowering his voice, "you want to end your career with a court-martial. Take it or leave it."

"I can't marry her, Colonel."

"You can't retire with a court martial on your record, either, John. I've always known you for a man of honor. Stubborn, maybe. Sometimes you march too much to your own drummer, but honorable, nevertheless. Now, you're going to make it right with that girl and that's that."

"Colonel—"

"Don't argue with me, John. This is the best thing I could have hoped for you. I'm just helping things along."

The fiddle suddenly started up with a burst of raucous music, and men raced to claim partners.

"Harry, listen—"

"You are dismissed, Major."

His mind reeling, John found himself heading across the floor, ignoring hands extended in congratulations, cooing women, even Nettie in her low-necked green dress, smiling as if she'd just swallowed a quart of cream. The need to be outside, away from this sham lengthened his stride.

Even after he had reached the parade ground perimeter and walked off his anger, he still couldn't think straight. He wanted to go to Constance. Wanted to saddle up and ride straight on to Idaho without stopping. He wanted...

The faint sound of Billy's fiddle floated to him on the night air, the melody so full of longing his heart closed in on itself.

And then he remembered Constance's face looking up at him, her mouth composed, her eyes shiny with tears. With understanding.

He didn't trust himself around Nettie at the moment. He'd like to shake that lying little bitch until her bones rattled. He didn't trust himself around Constance, either. He wanted to touch her. Bury himself in her.

With a low, anguished groan, he headed for Billy's camp and the rest of the whiskey.

Chapter Fourteen

Before the sun was up, Constance slipped out of her pallet under the wagon and pushed through the canvas bonnet. Nettie lay curled up under the blue patchwork quilt, her breathing soft and regular. The green dimity dress lay in a heap on the trunk lid, topped by a careless assortment of petticoats, underdrawers and a rose-embroidered corset cover.

"Nettie, wake up."

"I am awake, Cissy. I've been waiting for you."

Constance gazed down into her sister's wide blue eyes. "Have you, now?"

Last night after the dance she had walked three times around the parade ground perimeter to cool her fury. This morning she was still so angry her voice shook. "What on earth are you up to, Sister?"

Nettie returned her look with a defiant tilt to her

chin. "It is perfectly obvious, is it not? I am engaged to the major."

Constance stared at her. "You are no such thing."

"It's true. Colonel Butterworth said so. He announced it last night at the dance." Her voice became silky. "You were there, Cissy, and I know you heard."

"That does not make it true. Oh, Nettie, how *could* you?"

Nettie shoved herself up to a sitting position. "How could I what?"

"How could you brazenly entrap a man that way?"

"It wasn't brazen." Nettie's lower lip pushed forward.

"I told the colonel about my condition, and…"

"You lied to him! You made up one of your stories and tricked a well-meaning man with a complete fabrication."

"I did not lie. I merely hinted at a few things."

"Nettie, listen to yourself!"

Nettie's head came up. "What is so wrong about wanting to get married?"

"Nettie, people are not playthings, to be used when you need them and then tossed away. Other people have feelings, commitments you know nothing about."

"But…" Nettie began to snuffle. "I *must* get married, Cissy. I am carrying a child!"

"It is not Major Montgomery's child. You are just using him. And you manipulated Colonel Butterworth into helping you do it. Never, *never* have I been so distressed at your behavior. Your actions are selfish and arrogant and thoughtless beyond what I would have thought possible."

She turned away, unable to watch the tears puddling in Nettie's eyes. "You are my sister, but at this moment I cannot bear to look at you."

She snatched her brown everyday dress off its nail and dove underneath the skirt.

"Well, Cissy, have you asked yourself why you are so upset about my engagement? Perhaps you fancy the major for yourself?"

Constance popped her head through the neck opening. "A man is not a prize, like a horse or a cow, to be squabbled over. A man has feelings, too." She yanked the bodice into place and began on the buttons. Her hands trembled so violently she couldn't manage a single one.

"What if the major loves me?"

"He does not."

"He might. I've seen him look at me…"

"He does not," Constance repeated.

Nettie cocked her head and peered up at her. "You think he cares for you, is that it?"

The question caught her by surprise. Her heart somersaulted into her throat. "No. Oh, I don't know."

"That *is* it! I knew it. You're jealous, Cissy. Jealous!"

Constance flinched. Nettie was partly right. But only partly.

"I'm desperate, Cissy. And you're not. You have time to find someone else."

But this is the man—the only man—I want. The only man I have ever wanted.

"I don't want anyone else!" She flung the words at Nettie as if they were red-hot coals.

"Well, the major hasn't spoken for you, has he? And since he hasn't…well, he didn't object when the colonel announced—"

"I asked him not to humiliate you in public."

"And you want me to believe that's why he said nothing? That he did it for you?"

"I think rather that he did it for himself. Major Montgomery has good manners."

"Well, then, don't you see, Cissy? He will marry me, and we'll all be happy again, like it was before Papa died. Before…" Nettie gazed up at her with a stricken look on her face. "You must help me, Cissy, Please. *Please*. I cannot bear this alone."

Sick at heart, Constance knelt beside her. "Is it not enough that I love and care for you because you are my sister?" she said in an unsteady voice. "That I give you the food off my plate? That I would give my life to keep you safe? You want this, as well?"

"I do, Sister. I must have it, don't you see?" She buried her face against Constance's neck. Her skin was sticky with tears.

"Yes," Constance said, gentling her voice. "I do see. But it is not up to me. Nor even you, Nettie. The major is his own man."

"What do you mean?"

"In the end, it must be his decision."

For better or worse, it must be his decision. But, God in heaven, she would put nothing past Nettie now.

"Told ya so, Major. That Nettie's a cracker, all right."

John narrowed his gaze, scanning the long hill ahead of them. "It is not my intention to dance at the end of Nettie Weldon's rope."

"Huh. The road to hell is paved with such-like intentions. No man wants to be under a gal's thumb."

John said nothing.

"What Miss Nettie needs is a steady hand on the reins and maybe a thwack across her backside ever' so often."

"Not interested."

"Don't hafta be. She's got you hog-tied and halfway to the altar."

"No, she doesn't."

"Don't see it, do ya, Major? How some woman kin work it."

"No, I damn well don't."

"Well, listen to ol' Billy. I told ya right off, I did—remember, John? Told ya two unattached women on a wagon train usually means consternation with a capital *K*."

John reined up and pinned Billy with a look. "You've said enough, Billy."

"Sure, John. Sure. Didn't mean to rile ya up none." He sent John a sidelong glance.

John squinted into the sun and changed the subject. "See anything odd about that sycamore up ahead?"

"Gonna be one damn strange family, you and the sister, and the sister's sister. What sycamore?"

"Something dark around the trunk." The major kicked his mount. As they drew nearer, his frown dissolved into a grin.

"Billy, I'm going to ride on ahead. You drop back and get Miss Constance. She's not going to believe this."

"What is it? I don't see nothin'—oh, you mean that thingamabob tied around the base of that tree? Looks to me like…" Billy chuckled. "Sure, I'll go get her. Maybe this'll cheer her up a mite."

He peeled off and circled around behind the wagons, coming up on the left side of the big blue Conestoga Constance was driving.

"Good morning, Billy."

"Mornin', Miss Constance. Major wants to see ya. He's up ahead a ways."

Her smile faltered. "Will he wait?"

"Naw. You climb down and take my horse. I'll drive yer wagon."

"Go slowly, won't you? Nettie's asleep in the back."

Billy grinned. "Now, don't you worry none about Miss Nettie. She's in good hands."

Constance winced. Nettie was in the major's hands, if she took Billy's meaning. And there wasn't one blessed thing she could do about it.

She pulled the team to a halt, set the brake and climbed down. Billy dismounted, laced his fingers together and lifted her foot to help her mount.

"This here's a smart horse, Constance. Jes' a light touch on the reins is all you'll need."

"Thank you, Billy. The oxen, however, are tough hearted but steady. I don't use the whip much."

Billy grinned at her. "I've driven oxen. You've rid a horse. Seems like we're about even."

He watched her put the paint into a canter, and then a trot as she went forward to meet the major. "Damn fine woman," he muttered. "Major oughtta wake up pretty quick, or it'll be too late."

He lifted the whip. "Gee-up, you sons o' the devil. Make a track 'r two!"

She rode faster than she knew was safe on an unfamiliar mount, but something pulled at her. Within a few minutes she drew up to where the major's dark horse waited beside the trail.

"How are you, Constance?"

"Well," she said in a tight voice. "And you?"

His eyes sought hers. "Lying, just like you."

Constance studied his sun-browned face, the steady blue eyes that held hers with an unspoken message. "Yes, we are, aren't we?"

"Yep." His lips thinned. "Can't do much else, I guess."

"Yes," she said. Her heart began to ache as it

did every night, only now she was denied the release of tears.

She steadied her breathing. "You wanted to see me?"

"Yep. Look yonder." He pointed at the sycamore tree.

Something was tied around the trunk, like a daisy chain of various-sized dark objects. She stepped the horse forward.

"Moccasins! Why, they're beautiful! Where did they come from?"

"Yellow Wolf, I'd bet. Count them."

Constance bent from the saddle. "Seven pair. And all sizes, as if…"

"For the Ramsey children. And a pair for you and your sister. He probably measured all your footprints."

"Footprints?" The fine hair on her neck rose. "You mean Yellow Wolf is tracking us?"

"Not tracking, exactly. Just feeding himself on whatever he finds lodged in the crotch of a tree, and wanting to repay the baker."

Constance shot him a glance. "You saw me! You know what I've been…."

His lips twitched, and she felt an odd sense of relief.

"You're pretty damn smart." He dismounted in

an easy motion, flicked open a penknife and cut the leather thong that was wound around the trunk.

"Here." He handed up the string of deerskin slippers.

"Going barefoot on the Oregon Trail is rough on children. And ladies. Yellow Wolf meant to thank you."

The largest pair was covered with tiny blue and white beads. "I am touched, John. Yellow Wolf must be a good man."

The major pressed his lips together. "He is not a good man. Don't get careless and walk out alone."

"But you told him...he thinks I am *your* woman."

John remounted and caught the bridle of her horse, drew close enough to reach out and touch her if he wanted. But he did not.

"You *are* my woman. And Yellow Wolf is what he is. A thief."

Constance stared at him, her thoughts tumbling over themselves. *She was his. He wanted her to be his.*

But he was looking at her so oddly, as if...as if he was angry.

"So there it is," he said without inflection. "I don't know what we're going to do."

Her breath stopped. "We?"

"You and me." He released her horse and lifted his own reins. "I'll come to you tonight. We'll talk about it then."

He wheeled the mare away and rode on into the sun.

Chapter Fifteen

I cannot clear my mind tonight of all that has happened. Nor can I help but wonder what Papa must have endured in the weeks before his death. Mama's face, full of frowns and disapproval, haunts me daily. To think she worried over me—me!—simply because I talked the ears off most people. What a conniption fit she would suffer now.

I have thought of little else these past days but how sorely disappointed Papa must be that I have failed to keep Nettie from disaster. I feel powerless to change the circumstances, but Lord God, what should I do to protect Nettie now?

Major Montgomery has spoken little to me of late, and even less to Nettie, but rides far out in front of the wagons and at night walks off into the dark by himself. I cannot go on as we are.

* * *

Footsteps crunched toward the wagon beneath which Constance rested. Hurriedly she puffed out the candle stub and lay still, clutching her journal at her side. By the time her eyes adjusted to the dark, whoever it was had reached the Nylands' wagon next to hers, and here the footsteps paused. And then she heard another step, closer.

Boots. She breathed a sigh of relief. Not an Indian. Not Yellow Wolf. At least not wearing boots. And anyway, an Indian would not walk boldly right into a white man's camp, even if she had left loaves of bread for him. She had wrapped them in a towel and tied them to the sycamore with the same deer-hide thong that had laced the moccasins together.

The footsteps moved to the wagon and stopped. Constance peered out from underneath and recognized the scuffed black leather. Joshua Duquette.

She held her breath until he went on, and she let a full quarter hour pass before she dared to move.

The next thing she knew a hand slipped over her mouth.

"It's John," a low voice murmured. "Don't yell." Making no sound, the major slid his long length under the wagon next to her.

"Took me a while to get here," he said in an undertone. "I've been following Duquette on his walk-around, thought he'd never go back to his wagon. Then Mrs. Stryker got to coughing. Figured she'd wake up the whole camp."

"I heard Duquette," she whispered. "Then not another sound until you came."

"Old Indian trick. Wrapped my boots in deer-skin."

He barely breathed the words, keeping his mouth near her ear.

"Nettie's in the wagon, asleep."

"Maybe. I don't trust her. Kind of wondering why you still do."

"John, she's my sister."

He chuckled low in his throat. "Abel was Cain's brother. Didn't count for much."

"Oh, this is the worst mess I could ever have imagined. It is so awful it seems unreal."

He let out a long breath. "It's real, all right. At least what's growing inside Nettie is real. The rest of it, her playacting with Colonel Butterworth, reeks of deception."

"I don't know what to do." She forced the words past a hard, dry lump blocking her throat. "John, do you...do you have any whiskey?"

Again he chuckled, his breath ruffling her hair. "Well, that's one way. Sorry, but I drank it all that night the colonel announced my impending marriage."

Constance bit her lip. "I can't sleep at night for thinking of Nettie and what has happened."

"I can't sleep, either." He brought his hand up, laid his warm palm against the side of her face. "But not because of Nettie."

She drew in a shuddery breath. "John. Oh, John, what are we going to do?"

He rolled onto his back, covered his eyes with his forearm. "I can marry her. Give her child a name."

"Yes, you could do that. Or she could face up to what she's done and bear the child out of wedlock."

"Even out West, having a baby outside marriage will ruin a woman. Being her sister, you will be tarred by the same brush."

"I don't care. I don't care about me."

He uncovered his eyes and turned his face toward her.

"You must care. You will be settling out in Oregon, where a person is pretty much on his own. Especially a woman. Your actions, your good name will determine whether you end up being shunned or having friends and neighbors when you need them. Nettie can drag you both through the mud."

"Marrying her will ruin your life, John."

"Right now it's the only way I can think of to protect you."

She shut her eyes to squeeze back stinging tears. "I cannot bear to think of you with her. I know it sounds petty and selfish, but…" Her voice caught.

"I won't sleep with her. And I won't live with her. But it will accomplish something—it won't compromise *your* life. *Your* future. I'd do it for you as much as anything."

"I want no future without you. I told Nettie as much, but she said it doesn't matter."

"It doesn't, to her. It does to me. I never thought I'd feel anything for another human being, but I do. God help me, I do."

She waited until she could speak. "How far is Fort Laramie?"

"Eleven days. Maybe twelve. We've got some hills ahead of us, and some steep bluffs after that."

"Twelve days," she whispered. "Only twelve days."

"For the time being, it's all we've got."

She fought to think clearly. "Where will you live, if not with Nettie?"

"Fort Kearny. I'm a soldier, Constance. I have orders. When I'm free, I'll come for you."

"After Nettie's baby is born."

"Christmas, you said."

Her heart felt as if it were cracking right down the middle. "I want you to come now. To be with us. With me."

"Oh, God, Constance." He rolled toward her, gathered her into his arms. "I can't. I can't go on to Oregon right away, not without incurring a court martial. In August, I can muster out with pay. I'll come for you then. I'll catch up to the wagon train at Farewell Bend."

"It will be hard," she cried against his neck. "It's all upside down because of Nettie."

"It's the best we can do, given the circumstances."

"Is there a chance you might not come in August? Or even December, when the baby is born?"

"Not one chance in hell." He nudged her chin up and kissed her, slow and hard. "Wait for me," he murmured against her mouth.

She closed her eyes and reached for him, held on tight while his lips sought hers and her soul cleaved in two.

When she could breathe again, he was gone.

The long hill stretched before them, climbing so gradually it looked as if it led right into the sun. Constance lifted her head and scanned the worn tracks marking their route. "Up and more up," she murmured. How could it get baked day after day by this summer heat, yet still be so green?

"Near two miles long," Billy West had said. Two miles of pulling their overloaded Conestoga would kill their oxen. She glanced back at the cow, lumbering behind the train along with the Ollesen brothers' mares. Lordy, with all this jouncing, by evening Molly should give pure butter!

Nettie and four of the Ramsey brood straggled with listless steps to the left of the wagons, far enough ahead to be shaded by the Stryker's canvas bonnet but not out of earshot. All of them wore their new moccasins, even Nettie, whose fashionable black leather shoes now had two silver-dollar-sized holes worn through the soles. In the afternoon heat, their steps dragged, even though Nettie was urging them on with a game.

"And then the…?" She paused, waiting for an answer.

"Antelope!" Essie shouted.

"Good." Nettie ruffled the child's blond curls. "And then the antelope said to the…" She paused significantly and touched seven-year-old Elijah on the shoulder.

"Buh…bor…baby!"

Nettie missed a step. "Yes, that's a fine *B* word.

And the antelope said to the baby, 'Why do you have no horns, as I do?'

The alphabet game again. Constance listened in spite of herself. The next round would be Remembering and Counting Syllables, and then the children would spell out the words. Even four-year-old Essie knew all her letters and her numbers up to fifty. Given enough incentive, Nettie could teach a horse to speak French.

Ahead of them trudged heavyset Flora Stryker, her back ramrod stiff as she marched beside the wagon in her peculiar rolling gait. Her gray hair was tucked up under a blue prairie bonnet that matched her apron, and when she lifted her voluminous skirt to avoid a patch of wild roses, Constance glimpsed a bright red petticoat ruffle.

Well, the woman wasn't so old that she couldn't kick up her heels a bit! Mrs. Stryker had a ready laugh, and those days when Nettie felt faint with the heat, the old woman sent her to lie down in the wagon with a cool cloth over her eyes and watched over the children herself.

Today Nettie seemed fine. It was Flora Stryker who was having trouble breathing. Her wheezy cough carried back to Constance, and her own throat felt dry and raspy. She reached for the water canteen.

The wagons slowed to a crawl. She could see the long line of them snaking up the hill, the white canvas bonnets floating over the land. The lead wagon, Joshua Duquette and his wife, came to a complete halt, followed by the Nylands and on down the line. Constance pulled the team to a halt and waited.

Billy West rode back, stopping at each wagon. "Major says to unload yer heaviest piece so's you kin pull up yonder incline."

Nettie and Constance exchanged glances. "Not Mama's sideboard," Nettie moaned.

Constance tried to make her voice as matter-of-fact as possible. "It's either that or the chiffonier."

"But Cissy, the sideboard has all Mama's china and silver packed inside."

"The chiffonier has all our clothes and linen."

"Oh, I can't do it, Cissy. I just can't. We can't do without either one."

Ahead of her, the major and two other men settled a nickel-plated cookstove beside the Nylands' wagon.

"Everyone has to give up something to lighten the load, pet."

Nettie's lower lip came out. "Well, we shouldn't have to. We don't weigh as much as some people do." She shot a disparaging look at Mrs. Stryker. "I'll just speak to Major Montgomery."

Nettie had flounced no more than a dozen steps when Billy West intercepted her. "Care to ride, Miss Nettie? You kin use my horse iff'n you want privacy for a Necessary stop."

"I do not care to ride, thank you. I am going to talk to the major."

"Major's mighty busy, miss. Maybe you'll wanna talk to me, instead. I kin answer most questions."

"This is not a question," she snapped. "It is a request."

Billy pushed his dusty hat back and leaned forward. "In that case, go right ahead and request away."

"I do not wish to leave behind any of our furniture. These pieces belonged to my mother, and I do not wish to give them up."

"Sorry, Miss Nettie. Rules is rules. Better to unload something now than suffer a broken axle or a draft animal dyin' of a busted heart."

She sniffed and moved to go around him. "We'll just see about that."

Billy stepped the horse to block her way. "Now jes' hold up. I told ya the major's busy helpin' folks move their heavy pieces. I am speakin' for him."

Nettie reversed direction, started to whirl away from the horse, and Constance watched what happened next with widened eyes. Quick as a cat, Billy leaned down and snagged Nettie's apron tie. He dismounted, then reeled her in like a hooked trout.

A furious Nettie turned on him. "Just what do you think you're doing?" Her eyes blazed like two blue sapphires, but Billy didn't flinch.

"I'm teachin' you some manners, Miss High-an'-Mighty."

"*You're* teaching *me* manners? Don't be ridic—"

"Now you hush up an' lissen. You ain't so important that you don't hafta follow the rules like ever'body else."

Nettie slapped at the hand holding her imprisoned within her apron ties. "I am engaged to marry Major Montgomery," she said, her tone frosty. "Your superior officer," she added.

Billy yanked hard on the apron ties and Nettie's mouth closed with a little click.

"Way I see it, you've got a few things to learn about livin' in the real world. Fact that you're gonna marry the major don't make you special. Don't make *you* my superior officer, little girl."

"Doesn't," she corrected automatically.

"No, it don't." Billy raised his voice. "What about you, Miss Constance? You got a preference?"

Constance studied her sister's flaming cheeks, her delicately pointed but stubbornly raised jaw. She hated to see Nettie make a spectacle of herself. She would do almost anything for her, but in this matter the way was clear. They would have to give up something. They were no better, no more important, than anyone else in the train. The day they left Liberty Corners, their old, privileged life ceased. They were, all of them, simply emigrants going west.

Besides that, she knew their Conestoga wagon was larger and heavier than the others. "Take the chiffonier, Billy."

"Cissy!"

"We can always make new clothes, Nettie."

But inside her chest, her heart ached. Another link to their old life was breaking. The uncertainty of their future, of Nettie and the child she carried, tightened her belly into a hard knot.

At the same time, her conviction that obeying the major's orders and leaving the chiffonier behind was the only thing to do swelled until she wanted to weep with relief. It hurt, but it was the right thing to do.

How strange life was. Glorious and terrible all at the same time.

"Major," Billy yelled. "Over here."

The two sisters stood side by side and watched the major and Billy wrestle their mother's favorite rose oak chest out of the wagon and onto the grass beside the trail.

After a moment, Constance put her arm around Nettie's shoulders.

Chapter Sixteen

At the crest of California Hill, the major reined in his mount and watched the last of the eleven wagons creak past him.

"Dat iss one long pull," Arvo Ollesen gasped as he tramped by. His younger brother, Cal, leading the team of oxen that strained against the weight of their wagon, lifted his round-topped straw hat but said nothing. Winded, John guessed. They would all need to rest before the next challenge—winching the heavy wagons down the steep bluff just ahead.

The worst would be the Weldon sisters' blue Conestoga. Bigger than the others, the Conestoga was top-heavy to begin with, and was now loaded to the roof staves with trunks and barrels and that handsome sideboard, which alone must weigh a thousand pounds. He could guess what was packed inside—

china, hope chest linen, silver enough for two complete wedding trousseaus.

The thought brought a low groan out of his parched throat. He uncapped his canteen, tipped his head back and drank deep just as Billy reined up beside him.

"That water or whiskey?"

John handed over the container. "Water."

Billy handed it back. "No thanks. Need somethin' stronger. Haven't felt this blowed out since… 'member that time three, four summers ago up around—whatsa matter, Major? You look like you seed a ghost."

John squinted back down the long sloping trail they had just climbed. "Not a ghost, but something. There, behind that hill."

Billy shaded his eyes with a sun-browned hand. "Prairie haze, maybe. Or smoke."

"Or dust." The major dismounted, tossed a handful of dirt into the air and studied it as it sifted downward. "Wind's from the north. Could be buffalo. Maybe horses."

"Take a passel of horses to raise that kinda cloud. Whaddya thinkin', John?"

"I think we need to get off this hill." He remounted and turned his mare toward the lead wagon. "I'll talk to Duquette. You warn the others. Don't scare them, Billy. Just warn them."

"Right, Major."

"And Billy...we'll need good strong rope. All you can find."

The wagon master bellied up as close as he dared to where John sat his horse. "Are you crazy, Major? The animals are plumb tired out and we haven't stopped for nooning yet. The men are hungry."

"Can't help that, Duquette. We're too exposed up here."

"Took us the better part of the day to get up this here hill. It'll take twice as long to get down."

"It will probably take half the night, too, considering how steep it is ahead. Now, get moving."

"I'm damned if I will. No harm in campin' right here, where we're standin.'"

"Look behind me, Duquette."

Duquette peered past him. "Nothin' but a big cloud. Not even any lightning."

"That's a Cheyenne war party on the move."

The wagon master spat in front of the horse. "Now just how would you know that?"

"I've seen them before. They like to ride into the wind. They're heading this way."

The wagon master's face changed. "You sure about that?"

"You want to stay and gamble I'm wrong or get down to Ash Hollow and the shelter of some trees?"

"I ain't afraid to fight."

"There's women and children to consider. Move it, Duquette."

The stocky man stomped away, and John swept off his hat to rake his fingers through his hair. Billy rode up and waited, saying nothing, until John acknowledged him.

"Sooner or later, you 'n Duquette are gonna have it out, and it won't be pretty."

"You get enough rope?"

Billy grinned. "Plenty of rope. You wanna string somebody up?"

"Waste of good rope," the major growled.

"Then let's dangle a few wagons over the cliff. That'll give Duquette religion faster'n a deep-river baptism."

"Put the Ollesen brothers in charge of the animals, Billy. Tell them to drive them down easy to smooth out the path, then corral them back in that grove of trees."

Billy's grin widened. "'Member the time the rope busted an' we lost—? Oh, yessir, Major, I'm goin'."

He sent John a hasty salute and trotted off to help unhitch the oxen.

John stepped his mare to the edge of the bluff and studied the incline. He prayed that eleven men and fifty yards of rope would be enough. Ten men, he amended. Friedrich Stryker was too frail and unsteady on his feet to be much help.

The first wagon over the cliff was Joshua Duquette's. The wagon master and four other men dug in their heels and paid out the rope tied to the right rear axle and looped about their waists, sweating and grunting against the weight. Another team of four men, including Enos Ramsey and Billy, managed the left axle. Eliza Duquette stood on the butte, wringing her hands and moaning.

The Ollesen brothers ''caught'' the wagon at the bottom of the slope, hitched up a team to pull it out of the way, then hallooed to signal the winching teams above to send the next wagon.

The men worked until dark, when the only remaining wagon was the blue Conestoga. It was so heavy it took the eight men working the ropes with all their strength just to hold steady. The major added his muscle but still they couldn't hold on. Boots scrabbled and slid as the loaded wagon overbalanced them.

''Got to unload something more,'' the major

panted. The hemp around his waist began to slip, and the wagon teetered at the edge. "Somebody get Miss Constance," he gritted out. "Ask her—"

A clear, firm voice spoke from the knot of women onlookers. "Unload the sideboard."

"Oh, Cissy, no!"

"The wagon must be lightened, Nettie. We don't want to spend the night up here, just the two of us in our wagon. We must stay with the others."

"But…all of our dishes, and Mama's silver tea service, and… Oh, Cissy."

"Hush up, Nettie. We should worry about having enough food, not plates to put it on."

The men pegged the wagon so they could unload the sideboard. When the major and three other men levered the beautifully grained oak piece out onto the ground, Constance turned her face away.

Yes, Mama's silver. And the goblets she'd brought from England, the gold-edged plates, twelve of them, with the matching—

Her throat closed. She blinked back tears and met the major's steady gaze.

Nettie dashed across the short distance and threw herself against the major's chest. "All Mama's things," she sniffled. "Oh, my poor heart is just breaking."

Looking straight at Constance, the major set Nettie aside. "All our hearts are breaking. Nothing of value ever comes for free."

Constance turned away, biting the inside of her cheek to keep from weeping.

The ordeal was over at last. All the wagons, even the blue Conestoga, were safely assembled on Ash Hollow flat. Cooking fires flickered and smoked, bacon sizzled, the Ramsey baby squalled for its supper.

Suddenly Constance couldn't stand it one more minute. Snatching off her apron, she started for the makeshift corral the Ollesen brothers had rigged. She was too tired and too heartsick to roll out one more biscuit. Or listen to one more whined complaint. Nettie could cook her own supper.

How had she lived all these years with her sister and not noticed how self-centered she was?

Perhaps it was the baby she carried. Perhaps when a woman conceived, her whole self was filled up with...herself.

She found Molly tethered under an ash tree with a length of worn rope, contentedly chewing her cud. Constance leaned her forehead against the cow's warm hide and closed her eyes.

How many more days to Fort Laramie? Ten? Nine? Her mind was such a jumble she'd lost track. Nine, that was it. Once again they faced an unbroken plain, with no rivers to ford or steep canyon walls to descend using ropes and manpower. The unimpeded miles would roll by quickly.

Nine days until John married Nettie. Nine days and then she could no longer walk out with him at night to look at the stars, could not stand within the circle of his arms. Not touch him.

Molly flicked her tail and lowed. "Yes, girl. It's long past milking time, I know." And no matter how much her head pounded or her heart ached, the business of life had to go on.

Squaring her shoulders, she went to fetch the bucket.

After taking supper at the Ollesen camp, John mounted his horse, rode back up the slope to the top of California Hill and settled down to keep watch. It was too dark to see a dust cloud kicked up by a band of Indians. Too dark to see much of anything but the glow of campfires in Ash Hollow below. He noted that the Cheyenne—if they were Cheyenne— had lit no fires. Only a war party, without women and children, would take such a precaution.

If they *were* Cheyenne. To his knowledge no white man's army was in the vicinity except for the garrison at Fort Laramie, and that was a hundred miles farther west.

Sioux, maybe? No. Too far north.

Maybe not Indians at all, but stampeding buffalo? Yet there had been no noise.

John, you've got the un-easies, as Billy would say. The question is, Why?

Because things went too smoothly today, despite having to hand-winch eleven wagons down the rough side of a bluff?

Because Nettie Weldon made a fool of herself in front of the whole train and Constance just looked at him, her face calm and her eyes steady?

Something was going to happen, he could feel it at the back of his scalp. Yellow Wolf used to laugh at his "old woman's premonitions." That is, until the raid at Straw Creek.

Billy would say he felt nerve-peckish because he hadn't eaten enough of Arvo's venison stew.

Colonel Butterworth, damn the man's hide, would say he had bridegroom's nerves.

He peered into the dark until his eyes burned. Not a sound except the slow *scrick-scrack* of crickets and the bawling of a cow somewhere below him. Maybe it *was* just bridegroom's nerves. He wouldn't be the first man to have them.

He shook his head. But he might be the first to get married under threat of an army court-martial.

Damned meddling do-gooder. John had never compromised a woman in his life, and the colonel knew it.

He nudged the mare forward, let her pick her own surefooted way down the loose scree. At the foot of the hill he stopped to listen again.

A whippoorwill. A cow. A baby's cry. A woman singing "Rock of Ages" in a gravelly voice. Billy's fiddle, low and mournful. It made his insides ache. *God Almighty, it was Constance he wanted, not Nettie.*

He knew what it was like to lose a woman. He didn't think he could do it again.

To give himself something to do, he dismounted and started toward the corral.

"Look, mister Major, see what I found?" Ruth, or maybe her twin sister, Essie—he couldn't tell them apart—swished a curving black feather against his trouser leg. John went down on one knee to take a closer look.

"Yes, it's very pretty. Where did you find it?"

"On that tree over there. It was tied to a branch, way high up. I got my big brother Parker to reach it for me."

John's heartbeat tripled. "Which tree, honey? Show me."

She grasped his hand and tugged him forward.

"Sure as shooting," he muttered when he saw the

deer-hide thong had been laced around the limb of an already yellowing ash. "Been here and gone, and not too long ago."

He turned the child around. "Run home to your wagon, Ruth. It's time for—"

"I'm Essie," the child announced. "Can I keep my pretty feather?"

"Sure you can, Essie. Time for bed now."

"First, I'm gonna kiss you good-night." She brushed her small mouth against his raspy cheek and raced away.

John rose, his hand touching the spot. Good God, by Christmas he would have a child of his own to protect. And a wife, as well. But it wouldn't be Constance. Instead of joy, he felt despair roll over him.

He'd thought it out long and hard. It wouldn't be easy, but it would at least afford Constance a respectable future.

Not if you don't find her before that renegade Indian does. The feather was a sign that Yellow Wolf wanted to talk.

The thought drove him forward, toward the corral. Last he'd seen Constance, she was heading down to milk Molly.

She came up the path toward him, her head down, the milk bucket in her left hand. He lifted it away and set it down.

"I want you to sleep inside your wagon tonight."

"I can't, John. Nettie and I have such awful arguments."

"Then come to our camp, Billy's and mine. Yellow Wolf is around, wants to parley. Also might want to steal something."

Her hand went to her mouth. "Not the cow!"

He shook his head. "Not the cow. You."

"He wouldn't dare. Would he? He thinks I belong to you."

"I don't know what he thinks. If he was watching us today, saw Nettie and me—"

She gave a little gasp. "Watching us?"

"You know he's trailing us. Your bread's probably keeping him alive."

"Yes, I…I will come to your camp—oh, no, I can't. Nettie would be alone, and she gets frightened at night."

John put his hands on her shoulders. "Walk into those trees with me."

"But, John…"

"Walk," he said quietly. "We need to be private."

Well hidden within the copse of ash trees, John turned her toward him. "I think Billy and I will relocate our camp. Starting tonight, we'll roll our beds out on each side of your wagon. If anyone remarks on it, I'll tell them I'm protecting my fiancée. And her sister.''

"That is thoughtful of you, John. And generous. I know how much your privacy means to you."

"Not half as much as your life means to me. This way I can be sure you're safe."

She laid her palms on his forearms, moved her fingers over the warm skin. "Safe," she whispered.

"Safe. We both know that's going to have to be enough."

She looked up into his eyes. "It isn't."

"I know." He bent, kissed her mouth until they both trembled with wanting. "It's the best I can do, Constance. It's got to be enough, or I can't—"

"*This* is enough." She drew his head down to hers. "I cannot think beyond this moment."

"Maybe that's better," he said, his voice rough. "It hurts to look back, hurts to look forward." He waited three heartbeats before he could go on. "There's something I want you to know. Little Star was my wife."

"I know," she said in a soft voice. "I was never going to ask."

"I loved her."

"Yes."

"And I love you. I thought I was dead inside, that a woman would never matter to me again as long as I lived."

"You were wrong, John. And I am glad for it, even if we cannot—"

He stopped her words with his lips. She could feel him fight for control, then give up and hungrily take what she offered. His tongue was hot and smooth, and her thighs ached.

"Constance," he whispered. *"Constance."*

After a long, long moment, she stepped back out of his arms. Her entire body burned with hunger, with joy, with rage for what could not be hers. It was all so mixed up inside.

He put his hand at her back. "Come on. I won't feel easy talking with Yellow Wolf until I know you're safe and Billy's on guard." He retrieved the milk pail and they retraced their steps. Just before they reached the clearing where the wagons sat, he stopped and took her hand.

"There is more about Little Star."

"I guessed as much."

"I will tell you, when I am able."

"You need not, John. Ever. I will not ask."

"I want you to know, Constance. I will tell you when I can face it myself."

Chapter Seventeen

John moved on foot toward the whippoorwill's call, repeated at regular intervals from first one direction, then another. For the past fifteen steps he'd known it wasn't a bird; he was trying to pinpoint the location. Now he cupped his hands and signaled, then circled to his right.

A bent figure stepped out of the shadows ahead of him.

"Yellow Wolf, are you alone?" John watched the startled Indian whirl.

"I am alone, Brother. What warrior would ride with me?"

"What brings you?" John kept his tone neutral.

Yellow Wolf stepped toward him, cradling his twisted elbow with one hand. "I come to warn you. At sunrise, Cheyenne braves meet the Sioux on the plain to the north. Keep your wagons away from that place.''

"We travel westward tomorrow.''

Yellow Wolf raised his hand. "Do not,'' he said. "Keep your animals and wagons among the trees and your people hidden. I speak the truth if you have ears to hear.''

"I have ears, Brother. And eyes as well. Why do the Sioux seek their enemy the Cheyenne on the battlefield?''

"I would not know, John. I do not live among what were once my people. But I have walked many miles, and my eyes have seen much. Take care for your woman.''

"I will do so.''

"*Both* your women. This my eyes have seen also.''

"The two are sisters. I care only for one.''

The Indian's hard, black eyes shone for an instant. "The maker of bread? You do not deserve such a woman.''

"Perhaps not. I do what I think best.''

"You think to wash away your guilt. You will fail, Brother. And I will be glad.''

"I will not fail. You do not know my mind.''

"No one has ever known your mind, John. Not even Little Star.''

"You are wrong, Brother. She knew."

Yellow Wolf was silent for a long minute, squeezing his crooked elbow with long, crabbed fingers. "Tell your men to stay hidden."

"I will."

"Tell the women and the small ones nothing."

"I will not speak of it to the children. But I must—" He broke off. Yellow Wolf had slipped into the night, silent as a thought.

A weight settled over John's heart. Pressing at him. Punishing.

Something was about to happen; he could feel it in every bone of his miserable body.

"I said no, Duquette. I'm not going to say it again. Get your wagon back in place and douse that cook fire."

"Major, I've had about enough of you. Get out of my way."

"Not on your life. You take one step beyond the tree line and I'll drop you where you stand."

"Huh! With what? You ain't wearin' no sidearm. And in case you haven't noticed, I outweigh you by a good twenty pounds."

John said nothing.

"What's so dang important we got to wait all day to hitch up and roll?"

"I told you before, there's an Indian skirmish ahead of us."

"Sure there is, Major. Just in time for you to lay over a day and canoodle with yer—"

"Take your hand off that yoke, Duquette. Unhitch your oxen."

"Like hell. My hand's not gonna unhitch anything, 'cept maybe the damn coward standin' in front of me."

His fist snaked out and punched John hard in the solar plexus. His head snapped backward with the blow, and Duquette's hand slammed into his mouth. A sweet, metallic taste flooded his tongue.

When the wagon master came at him again, John was ready. He laced his two hands into one fist and dropped Duquette with a blow just above his jaw. The wagon master toppled like a poleaxed bull.

John stepped over the inert form and spoke into the wagon interior. "Better come out here, Eliza. Joshua's had an accident."

He strode off toward the wagons tightly packed in among the trees and dunked his throbbing head into the first water bucket he came to.

"Gottdam, Major, vat iss wrong?"

"Nothing, Arvo. Roll Duquette's wagon in close to the others and unhitch it, will you? Like I explained last night."

Arvo bobbed his blond head. "Sure, Major. Ve all keep quiet, like you say. Vill ve see anything, do you t'ink?"

"Not unless you want a Cheyenne arrow in your butt."

"I sit in wagon and read in my Bible, like quiet mouse. Cal, too, only he reads *Uncle Tom's House.*"

John splashed more water on his swelling lower lip and grunted. Arvo moved off to unhitch Duquette's team.

"You feed the animals so they won't bawl?" John called after him.

"Ya, sure," Arvo called over his shoulder. "Even the cow belonging to Miss Constance."

John leaned over the bucket. He'd walk down and refill it in the stream, then get Billy to doctor his lip.

And then...

Just what *was* he going to do with himself all day while Four Moons and a bunch of Sioux braves counted coups against each other just over the next rise?

When the sun reached the treetops, the travelers, except for Joshua Duquette, gathered in a ragged circle around Major Montgomery and ate a breakfast of cold biscuits and watery tea, listening to the major's final instructions.

"I want one armed man in each wagon, just in case some Indian brave loses his way and stumbles on to our encampment."

"How many rifles ve got, Major? Ve don't have none ourselves, vas using Mr. Duquette's."

"Count off," John ordered. "Sing out if you've got firepower."

Seven men responded.

"Only seven?" Billy spluttered.

"Eight counting Duquette," someone offered. "He's resting in his wagon. Got kicked by a horse, Eliza said."

"Makes nine all told, countin' my own muzzle-loader," Billy said. "Ten, countin' the major's side-arm. Cripes, that's all we got?"

"We have rifles," said a calm female voice at the back of the crowd.

"Cissy, we have no such thing!" a higher voice challenged.

"Yes, we do. Under the floorboards of our wagon."

The major shoved his hat back and sought Constance's eyes. "How many and what kind?"

"Three. Henry repeating rifles."

Billy's eyebrows did a little dance. "Henrys? You sure about that?"

"Quite sure. My father purchased them before we

left Ohio. He said they were not only protection, they were a good investment.''

''Well, I guess so,'' Billy chortled. ''By damn, three Henry repeaters. Hell, John, we could hold off the whole Sioux nation with three Henrys.''

John gestured to Constance. ''Show me. The rest of you men, divide up the weapons. It'll be a long, hot day of doing nothing but waiting, but keep them loaded and at the ready. Billy, come with me.''

The two men pried up the floor planks in the blue Conestoga with a crowbar. When the three canvas-wrapped boxes appeared, John gave a low whistle.

''Ain't never even been unpacked,'' Billy muttered.

''Ammunition?''

Constance pointed. ''That smaller box, in the back corner.'' Nettie hovered at her elbow, her eyes widening.

John lifted a polished blue-steel weapon from the nearest box. ''Your father show you how to fire one of these?''

''No!'' Nettie snapped. ''Of course not.''

''Yes,'' Constance countered, her voice quiet.

''Oh, Cissy, he didn't! You mean he showed you but not me?''

''Hush up, Sister. We will discuss it later. Right now, we have more important matters to consider.''

Nettie's lower lip came out. The gesture was so predictable, Constance almost laughed out loud.

"Billy, take one of these rifles and a box of cartridges to the Ollesens and another to Enos Ramsey. Tell Enos not to let it out of his sight."

"Sure thing, Major."

"Then come back here and give Miss Nettie a quick lesson in reloading your muzzle-loader, and keep a sharp eye on both of them unless you hear my signal."

"Yessir. Where'll you be?"

"I'll take one of the Henrys up on the bluff and keep a lookout."

"Y'er a settin' duck up there, John."

"Not flat on my belly with the sun at my back. You keep people quiet and out of sight. At least if some war party strays, I'll see them first."

Billy's eyes narrowed. "I don't like it."

"I don't much like it myself. Can't be helped."

Billy jerked his head toward the canvas bonnet. "Kin we talk this over private-like?"

John walked with him a few yards away from the Conestoga. "What's on your mind?"

"Been thinkin' things over. You ain't lookin' to get yourself killed, are you, John?"

"It's crossed my mind once or twice. But not today."

"There's some might say you got cause, both because of Little Star and now yer entanglement with Miss Nettie. Personally, I wish you'd be careful as a stiff-legged widow in a high wind."

"I'm not looking for a way out, Billy. I've got military orders to carry out."

"Yeah? Well, watch yer back. An' don't be so damn brave we have to get up a burial detail."

The two men exchanged a long look, and then Billy nodded and touched his cap. "I'll watch out for both of them. Be kinda fun, maybe. All that female talk and arguin' and tears and more arguin' and…come to think on it, you sure you don't want to send *me* up on lookout?"

John chuckled, slapped his hand on Billy's shoulder, and strode off to check the corral lines before he climbed the hill. Animals could get restless penned up all day.

By dusk, the camp itself was growing restless. Cooped up in the oppressive heat with nothing to do but worry about Indians on the warpath drove tempers to the boiling point.

Constance tried to mend the fraying hem of her work dress while Nettie alternately sulked and complained.

"It's so stifling hot in this wagon, Cissy. I can't stand it another minute."

"Make yourself a fan. Even a tea towel will do, but stop twitching. And stop whining."

"You don't care a fig about what happens to me, do you? Do you, Cissy? I'm all tired out and I feel one of my sick headaches coming on, and you just sit there cool as you please without one thought for me."

"Oh, for heaven's sake, Nettie, I am most certainly not cool. I am just as hot and sticky and discouraged as you."

Nettie shot her an interested look. "I didn't say I was discouraged. I said I was tired. Actually, I am not at all discouraged, as I have so much to look forward to—the wedding and all."

Constance laid her sewing in her lap. "Why are you doing this, Nettie? You don't love the major."

"I'm doing it because...because I don't want anybody else. He is so tall and...well, manly."

"You know absolutely nothing about him."

"Maybe not," her sister said with a jerk of her chin. "But I need somebody to marry, and soon, before many more weeks go by. I decided I want *him.*"

"It's wrong of you."

Nettie's eyes flashed. "What's so wrong about it?"

"You don't care for him."

"And I suppose you *do?*" Her lips curved in a triumphant smile.

"Yes," Constance said in a careful voice. "I do."

"Well, you can't have him. He's engaged to me, and Colonel Butterworth promised...well, he promised...things. I need the major, Cissy. Don't you see?"

Constance set the skirt aside, closed the lid of her wicker sewing basket and stood up. "I cannot listen to this any longer. I am going for a walk." She pushed through the bonnet without looking back.

"Where ya goin', Miss Constance?"

"Down to the corral, Billy. Molly will need to be milked." She lifted the bucket off its nail.

"Fresh air'll do you good. That an' a good cry, maybe. I'll keep an eye on Miss Nettie. You stay in the trees, you hear?"

She didn't answer. Couldn't answer, what with her throat already clogged with tears. Her vision blurring, she made her way between the close-quartered wagons and set off to visit Molly.

He saw a movement below him and raised his head. His old leg wound ached almost as bad as his back, but John kept his hands on the rifle instead of rubbing at the pain. When night fell, he'd make a poultice and find some whiskey. By then the war parties would be gathering their dead and dispersing.

He listened hard, but heard nothing but the wind. Even the whinny of a war pony would tell him where they were.

A cow bawled.

And then he saw Molly trailing her broken tether rope and heading for an open patch of grass, and Constance, a milk bucket in her hand, step out from the trees in pursuit.

Two Sioux braves on spotted ponies saw her, too. One of them nocked his bow and raised it.

Not again. Oh, God, not again.

Constance dropped the bucket and began to run.

Chapter Eighteen

John stood up, shouting to draw the attention of the two Sioux braves. One, wearing a feather war bonnet and red breechclout, glanced up, scowling through his ocher war paint. The other's gaze remained fixed on Constance.

John raised the rifle.

The Indian flexed his bow, pivoting his body to keep the arrow aimed true as Constance zigzagged toward the shelter of the trees.

The war bonnet tipped up toward him, and John heard a gutteral yell. Another mounted brave appeared, brandishing a spear and pounding toward the archer, who held his position.

Constance tripped, scrambled to her feet, and ran on. John squeezed off a warning shot, kicking up dust under the archer's pony. Neither man nor horse moved.

Don't make me kill you, you bastard. He fired again, purposely nicking the archer's calf. The only movement he saw was the slight lift of the Indian's right hand as he released the arrow.

The shaft flew straight and struck without a sound. Constance staggered but kept going.

John fired once more, this time aiming for the heart, but the horseman jerked his mount and raced away with his companions.

He skidded and stumbled his way down the bluff, already planning what he had to do. "Billy!" he shouted when he was within hearing distance.

"I've got her, John. She's bad hurt."

He ran toward the voice. "Got to get the wagons out of here," he panted. "Arvo, Cal, hitch up and get rolling!"

When he was sure Arvo had understood him, he pulled himself into the back of the Conestoga. "Constance?"

Nettie turned a tear-splashed face toward him. "She can't hear you, Major," she said in a quavery voice. "She made it to the corral, and Billy carried her the rest of the way. She…she has an arrow stuck in her back."

He knelt beside the still form on the pallet. Her face was white as flour paste, and blood darkened the bodice of her dress.

"Billy said her heart sounded steady, but...Major, she isn't going to—?" The thump and clank of oxen being yoked up carried over Nettie's question.

"Nettie, we have to move on, do you understand? The Indians rode off, but they will return now that they've seen us."

Nettie wrapped both arms over her stomach and rocked forward.

"Draw a bucket of water from the stream and see if you can catch Molly."

She shrank away. "I can't. I'm deathly afraid of cows."

John straightened. "I don't care if you're paralyzed with fear, just do it. March your feet out of here and do something to help!"

"If...if you say so, Major."

"On your way, ask Flora Stryker to come sit with your sister. We'll travel until full dark, that's about three hours. Maybe get ten, twelve miles farther west before we camp."

He watched Nettie stumble through the canvas opening, heard her scramble to the ground and speak to someone. A male voice answered.

"Arvo, that you out there?"

"It's Cal, Major. Arvo's helping Mrs. Duquette hitch their team."

"Shouldn't have hit Joshua so hard," John muttered.

"Didn't hit him near hard enough," Cal replied. "I'm finished here, Major. I go help Mr. Stryker."

John smoothed his palm over Constance's clammy forehead. She opened her eyes.

"John," she gasped. "Hurts."

"I'll get you some whiskey."

"No." She drew in an uneven breath and closed her eyes again. "On second thought, yes."

"Constance, we've got to move on. I don't have any laudanum, but—"

"Some in our pantry," she murmured. "Labeled Vinegar. I'd rather have whiskey. Have nice thoughts with whiskey."

John stared at her. "You've drunk whiskey before?"

"Not often. When Mama died. Papa, too. Helped."

He took her hand, lifted it gently in both of his.

"Constance, I hope it helps this time. It'll be rough. Your shoulder is going to hurt."

"Already does. How long?"

"Three hours. Maybe less."

"Will they follow us?"

"It's possible. The closer we get to Fort Laramie,

the more chance they'll have of running into an army patrol.''

"What will happen next, John? To me, I mean?''

Oh, God. But he had to tell her.

"When we stop, I'm going to get you so drunk you'll think you've gone to heaven." He swallowed. "And then I'm going to dig that arrow out of your shoulder.''

"Let Nettie help,'' she murmured. "She needs to belong. Be part of things.''

He squeezed her fingers. "Billy'd be better, but…all right.''

"Promise?'' Her blue-white lips formed a shaky smile.

John kissed her forehead, then gently brushed each closed eyelid with his mouth. "I promise.''

It took another three-quarters of an hour to get all eleven wagons on the trail. The lengthening shadows made it hard to see the wheel ruts that outlined the trail, but the draft animals seemed to know where they were going. The oxen plodded steadily forward, and night descended with no slowing of their pace. A scrap of moon lit their way.

In the Duquette wagon, Eliza sat on the driver's bench and carried on a desultory conversation with the still-wobbly wagon leader, who was reclining inside.

In the Ramsey wagon, four children slept, including the baby, and two of the older children—Parker and Essie—played a guessing game Nettie had taught them.

In the blue Conestoga, Flora Stryker sponged off Constance's face and Nettie sniffled. Billy West drove the oxen, gritting his teeth at the piteous sounds Nettie made. How come women couldn't cry in a way that didn't wrench up a man's insides?

John rode beside the wagon, leading Billy's horse and wondering if his companion had another bottle of whiskey stashed in his saddlebag. Molly, tied to the wagon with a new length of rope, bawled to be milked. Could Nettie…?

He thought not. Nettie's skills lay in other areas. Still, she'd surprised him by catching the cow. When they stopped to make camp, he'd get Billy to teach her.

By the time the moon set, there was just enough light to select an overnight spot and not a sign or a whisper of an Indian. Not even Yellow Wolf.

For the first time since morning, John let himself slow down. He even decided to risk a campfire. He'd need boiling water for the surgery.

It did not take long to set up camp, with John and Billy helping the Ollesen brothers unhitch and feed the oxen. Under Flora Stryker's supervision, Nettie dug a fire pit and put a kettle of water on to boil, as the major had instructed. Then, with Billy's help, she managed to milk Molly and set the cream to rise.

John realized he'd done nothing but bark orders all night when Billy took him aside.

"Un-rile yourself, Major. I know you're worried over Constance, but everything's under control. Even Nettie's behavin'. Why, she pulled those teats like she'd been born to it. Reminds me of the time, you remember, John, when we was chasin' Red Cloud into the Colorado badlands an' we came upon that wagon with the gut-shot—"

John turned away. "Billy, you talk too damn much."

Billy gave him an injured look. "Well, course I do. Hell, you never say a word to ease your worry, just clamp yer jaw shut and soldier on. So I'm showin' you the means to let off a little steam now'n again. Help you live long enough to—"

"Billy, so help me, will you shut up!"

"Nope. Not yet, anyway. Loosen up, John, or you're gonna botch what's gotta be done, and then she'll be scarred for the rest of her—okay, okay. That's my last word. My very last word."

John jerked his thumb at the kettle of water now

bubbling over the fire, and Billy grabbed a tin pan and filled it. John unpacked the surgeon's kit from his saddlebag, tore off his shirt and scrubbed his hands and arms until they stung.

Then both men moved toward the wagon.

Inside, Nettie sat next to Constance, dipping a folded cloth into cool water and bathing her pale face.

"Thought she needed somethin' to do with herself," Billy murmured. "Pretty hot in this here wagon."

John crouched beside the pallet. He hesitated, then gently touched her shoulder. "Want some more whiskey?"

Constance moaned.

Billy sent him a sideways look. "She's had near half that pint you left, Major. Gonna have an awful headache come morning."

"Can't be helped." He lifted her eyelid, assessed the pupil. "Give her half a cup more. I don't want her to feel much."

Nettie fluttered at his elbow. "You're not going to hurt her, are you?"

John stiffened his shoulders. "Got to."

Billy hunkered down on his other side. "See, Miss Nettie, it's this way. Arrow's gone almost all the way through. Cain't pull it backwards, so the major's gonna have to...well...push it forward so he kin grab ahold of it and—

Nettie sat down suddenly and leaned forward. "I think I'm going to be sick."

"No, you ain't, little girl. You buck up now and pull yourself together, like you done milkin' Molly."

"I don't think I can," came the shaking voice.

"Don't you never say that," Billy snapped. "Yer sister needs you to help us out here, so you jes' make up your mind to it. Y'all ain't gonna faint, 'r toss up your breakfast 'r cry."

"Aren't going to," Nettie corrected automatically.

"Damn right. Y'all ain't gonna do none of them things. You're a brave little filly, Miss Nettie. I seed it right off."

John shut his ears to Billy's gabble and snapped open his penknife. "I've got to roll you toward me, Constance. I'm going to cut away your dress."

Constance downed the last swallow of whiskey and reached for his forearm. "Can't. Hurts too mush." She opened her eyes wide. "Why, John, you don' have your shirt on!"

Sweat started down his back. "Pretty quick you won't have yours, either. Now, hold on to me."

He slid his hand to her back and rolled her forward. He heard her breath hiss in, and he tried to work fast, slicing down the back of the garment. He cut the blood-stiffened sleeves away, then worked the two pieces forward over one shoulder. She screwed her eyes tight shut and groaned.

Behind him Nettie stifled a sob.

"Nettie, help me get this off her."

She knelt across from him, dabbing at her eyes with the hem of her skirt. In the next minute, Billy settled next to her.

"Hold this," John said. He folded Nettie's fingers around a scrap of the bloodstained fabric. "When I move her, pull that piece forward and away. If you don't think you can do it…"

"She can do it," Billy rasped.

"Billy, bring that basin with my instruments."

He began to talk to her, hoping the sound of his voice would help. "The arrow's got to come out front-ways, Constance. Billy broke off most of the shaft when he carried you in, but the head's gone in pretty deep." He touched a finger lightly to her upper chest. "I'll try not to hurt you any more than I have to."

"John?" she murmured.

He bent, bringing his ear close to her mouth.

"More whishkey."

"In a minute." He peeled away the blood-soaked garment, slit it free of the arrow shaft.

"Now," she whispered.

He held the bottle to her lips and dribbled in a scant tablespoon. Before Constance finished swallowing, Nettie lifted the bottle out of his hand and gulped down a mouthful.

"Jesus," Billy blurted. "We'll all be drunk as skunks by the time this is over."

He set the steaming instrument basin on the floor near John's knee. The steel scalpels clanked inside the container.

Chapter Nineteen

"**I**'m going to do this in three stages, Constance. First I have to make an incision here—" he brushed his forefinger under the bone of her shoulder "—then push the arrow on through. The incision will prevent the skin from rupturing and the head will emerge clean. Then I'll pull it on through from the front."

He let out a slow breath. "I won't lie to you, Constance. All of it's going to hurt."

The ghost of a smile crossed her lips. "How d'you know all thish, John?"

"Happened to me, once." He stripped away the last shreds of her chemise and covered her breasts with a towel.

"Ish that how you got that scar on your shest?"

"That's how, all right," Billy interjected.

She studied the major's bare chest. "Will my scar look like that?"

"Better. Your scar will be smaller. And it'll be straight."

"Yours ishn't. Why ishn't yours straight, John?"

"Because my damn fool surgeon forgot to make the incision before he shoved the arrow through. Skin tore."

"I did no such thing," Billy sputtered. "You wouldn't let me near yer fancy scalper—"

"Scalpel," John corrected.

"—an' besides we had to keep movin', so there weren't no time to—"

"Oh," Nettie moaned. "Don't talk about it."

"Put yer hands over yer ears, then. We're just tryin' to put the patient at ease, ain't we, Major? 'Sides that, a little real talk is 'xactly what you're needin', missy."

John picked a shiny scalpel from the basin, and Nettie covered her face with her hands.

"This part's going to sting, Constance. Try to hold still." He blotted his forehead against his arm. "Billy?"

Billy reached over and wiped a cloth over John's face.

"Hold her hand," John murmured.

Billy slid his callused palm under Constance's fingers. "Jes' squeeze on me, hard as ya want."

She nodded.

"Ready?" John said, his voice barely audible.

She nodded again and shut her eyes. "I'm ready."

"Can you remember the words to 'Oh, Susanna'?"

"Of coursh. 'Oh, I come from Alablam…'bama, wish my banjo—"

He cut on the word "banjo." She sucked air in between her teeth but made no other sound.

"Good girl," John murmured. He sponged away the welling blood and laid the scalpel aside. "Now, I need you to roll toward me again. Billy will support you while I…"

Oh, hell, maybe I shouldn't tell her everything.

"G'wan, do it," Constance muttered. "Billy, where's your hand?"

"Easy, now. Nettie, grab her other hand."

When they moved her, Constance bit her lip and the color drained from her face.

"She's ready, John. Do it quick." Billy nudged the lantern closer, but his hand shook so hard the light wavered.

John grasped the handle of a flat-headed steel hammer and straddled her front-ways, her head bent into his chest. He'd have to do it in a single blow; she couldn't stand two.

He leaned over, lined up the hammer head with the broken arrow shaft and drove it in with all his strength. She jerked violently, and her muffled cry sliced straight into John's gut. He'd hurt her. It had to be done, but he'd hurt her. Tears stung under his eyelids.

And it wasn't over yet.

He looked down her backbone, felt her fingers claw into his thigh. Lord God in heaven, sometimes he wished he'd never seen a surgeon's kit.

He slid his palm to the back of her neck. "Lay her down, Billy. Slowly."

When she was prone, he tilted his head up to let Billy mop his face, then bent to listen to her breathing.

"Wha' about 'nother shong? I know lot of othersh."

For a moment he wanted to laugh. He'd never joked when Billy worked on *him*.

I wish Father had known her. He would have admired her, too. And loved her.

When his heart stopped pounding, he checked the wound. The arrow tip poked out from the neat incision he'd made in her chest. So far, so good. He swung his leg over her and straddled her again.

"Must you...sit on her like that?" Nettie asked in a watery voice.

"Need the leverage," he said. He hoped to God she wouldn't understand.

"Here's yer pliers, Major. Good luck."

"Pin her," John ordered.

Billy turned Nettie's face away with his free hand and pressed his knees down on Constance's shoulders.

"Talk to me, John." Her whisper tore into his gut.

"Please, please. I don' care what you have to do, jush talk to me while you're doing it."

John and Billy exchanged a look. He opened the plier jaws, fit them over the buffalo bone arrowhead and closed both hands around the handles.

"When I was growing up in Pennsylvania, my father set a trap for the fox that had been bothering our chickens...."

"You had schickens? Thash funny, John. Can't 'magine you gathering—"

He pulled on the arrowhead with all his strength, slow and steady, and he didn't dare let himself stop or look at her face. It came, slowly, with a sucking sound, and he tried to listen to that instead of her screams.

"Ya got it, Major. Just keep pullin'."

The shaft broke free with a little popping sound. Nettie stared, ashen faced, first at the major and then at her sister.

"Cissy?"

"Yesh, pet?" She spoke through tightened lips.

"Cissy, are…are you all right?"

Constance opened her eyes and tried to smile at John. "Jush fine, shister. John's gonna tell me 'bout his schickens, aren't you, John?"

Billy lifted the pliers and the arrow tip out of the major's trembling hand. "Done good, Major. *Ma'heono*." It was the Cheyenne word for strong medicine.

Constance looked up at him, trying to focus her gaze. "How many schickens did you have?"

He put his face next to hers, brought his lips to her ear. "You are the goddamnedest woman," he whispered. "Seven. I had seven chickens."

He finished the story about the fox while he cleaned the wound and made eleven neat stitches with surgical silk to close it. Nettie sat nearby, ripping a clean petticoat into bandages. Constance noted dizzily that it was one of *her* petticoats, not Nettie's, but she was too drained to smile over her sister's unthinking habit of putting herself first.

John's fingers bound the strips tight about her

shoulder and under her arm. When his strong, sure hands finished their task, she was regretful. Well, maybe not too regretful, for it had hurt more than she ever dreamed anything could. She wouldn't have been able to stand it had it been someone else's hands.

She liked the feeling she got in the pit of her stomach when he touched her. Especially now, when the pricking of his needle had stopped and he patted and smoothed and pressed the muslin strips over her wounds, front and back.

Her elbows felt as if they were floating above the pallet, and when she tipped her head, the candle lantern, the wagon, even John's face revolved around her. The effect made her giggle. He looked so serious, kneeling over her, his mouth tight, his dark eyebrows drawn into a frown.

And without his shirt. She suppressed another giggle, or thought she did, but he straightened suddenly and looked into her face.

"What's so funny?"

"You," she managed. "Everyshing. Nettie's— my—petticoat put to sush a purpose. John, let Nettie hold the lantern."

Billy cleared his throat. "Hold it up high, so's the major kin see what he's doin'."

Nettie eyed the tin box but made no move to pick it up.

"I don't need the light," John said. "I'm finished here."

"Oh, good." Nettie sighed dramatically. "I'm so exhausted I don't think—"

"Get up, little girl," Billy said in an oddly quiet voice. "Go on over to the Stryker wagon and eat some of Flora's stew, so's you can bring some back for your sister. She's a mite more exhausted than—"

"Billy, please," Constance breathed.

"You don't need me no more, Major, I'll take Miss Nettie on over and help her lift up her spoon."

Constance laughed out loud. "You're a good man, Billy. An' a good friend. Now, don't fret, Nettie. Go and eat."

John waited until the footsteps faded before he lifted Constance's hand in his and leaned close. "You sober?"

"Shertainly not."

"You hurting?"

She nodded. "Shoulder."

He fashioned a sling from a flour sacking towel, passed the long end around her bare neck and pinned it in place.

"You'll need help getting dressed tomorrow."

"Nettie can…"

"Wear something loose. Something like a man's shirt."

"Papa's dressing gown—oh, no, it was packed in the chiffonier we left behind."

He gave her a wry smile. "All your clothes are in the Ollesens' wagon. I unloaded the chest."

"John, you didn't? You did? You really did? I had no idea it would mean so mush—much—to me, but…" She hesitated. "Why did you do that?"

He looked away and began gathering up his instruments. "I wanted to save something for you out of the mess we're in."

She caught his hand and held it until he looked at her. "Thank you, John."

"I'm—" He cleared his throat. "I'm going to brew some willow bark tea for you. Indians swear by it."

"John…"

"Don't say it."

"You know, don't you? That I love…"

"Yes," he said quickly. He piled the instruments in the speckled tin basin and tried to keep his hands steady. "If I know Billy, he'll have the water on the boil and the tea pouch laid out. It tastes bitter, so you'll want some sug—" He stopped suddenly.

"The sugar's in the pantry, John."

He bent down, cradled her face between his two hands. "You'll have a helluva headache tomorrow."

"What d'you preschribe, Dr. Montgomery? More willow tea?"

"Coffee. Strong and black." He brought his lips to her cheek. "But if I could, I'd make it my whole heart and soul."

Chapter Twenty

"Cissy? Cissy, are you awake?"

Constance tried hard to open her eyes. "What is it, pet?"

"Cissy, I'm frightened."

"You've been frightened since we left Independence."

"I—I know. And it isn't Mr. Nyland's snoring or milking the cow, it's…"

Constance opened one eye. "Both the major and Billy West are sleeping right outside this wagon, Nettie. There is nothing to fear."

Nettie snuggled closer. "Lying here in the dark like this, it's like when we were young, isn't it? When I'd get scared at night and you'd let me crawl into bed next to you, remember, Cissy?"

"I remember." Constance squeezed her sister's small hand. "What has frightened you tonight?"

Nettie sighed. "Oh, lots of things. I thought you might die earlier."

Constance smiled. "I thought so, too, for a while. For a while, I wished I *would.*"

"But just think, Cissy. What would happen to me if you died?"

Her other eyelid snapped open. "You'd learn how to cook and churn butter," she said dryly. "Honestly, Sister, is your concern always for yourself alone?"

"N-no. But if you died all of a sudden, like Papa…"

"You would grow up, Nettie. The way I did when Mama died. You would have to."

In the long silence that followed, Constance patted the lump curled up under the quilt with her good hand and let her eyelids close. "Go to sleep, Nettie."

"I can't. I'm still worried about…something."

Constance heard the whiny tone Nettie used when she wanted something. "After what we have survived, what more could possibly worry you?"

Another silence.

"I don't have a dress to be married in," Nettie blurted. "Mama's wedding gown was packed away in the chiffonier. I was planning to wear it."

Constance sat up, clamping her jaw against the

pain in her shoulder. "You are worried about Mama's wedding gown? That's all?" She realized her voice would carry out into the night, but she didn't care. She couldn't stop herself.

"Not Indians on the warpath or Friedrich Stryker's weak heart, or how we will manage on wash day when I have use of only one arm? *Mama's wedding gown?*"

"Well...yes," Nettie said in a small voice. "And..."

"At least you are honest," Constance snapped. "And what?"

"And whether it will still fit in the waist, since I am...you know."

Her head spun. This time it had nothing to do with drinking too much whiskey. "Nettie, how *can* you be so...?"

But she knew how. Nettie had been spoiled and pampered all her life, and Constance now saw that she was as much to blame as Papa. She could be angry, furious, even. But she could not blame her sister for simply being the person she had been encouraged to be.

Nettie sniffled. "Cissy, don't be angry." Her small hand crept into Constance's. "I know you fancy the major, but if I don't get married quickly,

I won't fit into Mama's dress. Don't you see? You don't need someone the way I do.''

So furious she couldn't think clearly, Constance counted her breaths until she could speak. ''As for my not needing him, Sister, I would advise you to look beyond your own nose for once in your life.'' The words came out in a voice she had never heard herself use before.

''And, Nettie, here is something I do not want you to forget. Major Montgomery is not just 'someone.' If you ever, *ever* are unkind to him, or mistreat him in any way—in any way at all, do you hear me?— you will answer to me. Is that clear? Nettie?''

''Y-yes.''

''Then do not ever speak of him in this manner again. You will have Mama's wedding dress. Now, hush up, Sister, or I will cry, and it hurts me even to breathe!''

She stifled a wild impulse to get away from Nettie, climb out of the wagon, no matter how much it hurt, and walk out under the stars. John might be there.

And that, she thought when reason returned, was exactly why she could not.

John awoke to the enticing smell of coffee and sizzling bacon. For a moment he couldn't remember where he was, but then Billy's raspy voice came from the direction of the cookfire, singing in his peculiar musical style, half humming, half speaking.

"'...too long in the saddle, down Mexico way, the girls were all pretty, but I could not stay...'"

John winced. He'd listened to that particular song through most of Idaho and Montana, and it always brought back the same memories—two green army men who forged a friendship during a thousand-mile trek. He'd grown to hate the song, but he loved like a brother the man who sang it.

"'...and so I kept ridin', o'er valley and hill, and someday I'll find her, and wed her I will...'"

"You'll find," Billy remarked as he forked over a strip of bacon, "that women will surprise you. Yessir, when you think you know what they gonna do, they—"

John rolled over. "Billy?"

"'...up and say somethin' or smile atcha or start...'"

"Billy, who are you making this speech to?"

"Nobody in partic'lar, Major. Jes' thinkin' out loud."

"Think more quietly. You'll wake the women."

"Don't think so, Major. Nosiree. Miss Nettie and Miss Constance already up an' dressed and off to the necessary."

John sat up so fast his head swam.

"Ain't speakin' to each other, after last night, but they walkin' side by side like civilized folks." He dumped a cup of cold water into the bubbling coffeepot. "Though Miss Constance, now, she's pretty unsteady on her pins."

"What about last night?"

"Major, you slept through one of the purtiest speeches I ever heard, Miss Constance telling Miss Nettie a few things she had on her mind."

John pulled the tan buckskin shirt over his head, jammed his feet into the boots he'd used for a pillow and stood up. "Which way did they go?"

"I'd go th'opposite way if I's you, John. You're already in between 'em up to yer neck."

"Mind your own business, Billy."

"That's just what I'm doin', John. Coffee's ready."

John chuckled in spite of himself. Billy was right. He was in up to his neck, and coffee wasn't going to help.

Billy filled a cup anyway. "'…too long in the saddle down Mexico…'"

"Duquette been by?"

"Nope. Don't expect him, neither. He's waitin' to see what you're gonna do next. Here, Major." He handed John a speckled mug of thick black coffee. "My special brew."

"Whiskey?"

"Brandy. Found it in yer saddlebag when I stowed yer medical kit last night."

John put the cup to his lips. It smelled so rich and sweet it made his eyes water. "Billy, I'm going to recommend you for promotion."

The skillet banged onto the fire grate. "Don't even think it," Billy shot. "I don't want to be no closer to hell than I already am." He shoved a plate of food into John's hand. "Eat yer breakfast."

Three fluffy white biscuits looked up at him through a latticework of crisp bacon strips. "You make these?"

"You see anybody else with an apron tied around their middle? Miss Constance, she tried to help, but she cain't hardly see straight this mornin', let alone use that arm."

"There's always Nettie," John remarked. He crunched a piece of bacon between his front teeth.

"Yup. There's Nettie, all right."

And that was the last Billy offered on the subject.

They ate their meal standing up. When the two women returned to camp, Billy served them generous portions and set Constance's plate on an overturned box so she could try eating left-handed. John noticed she avoided direct sunlight, shielding her face, even under the wide-brimmed straw hat, with her hand in between bites.

"Head hurt?"

"Yes." She was careful not to nod.

"Here." He handed her his mug of brandy-laced coffee. "Hair of the rattlesnake."

"Don't make me laugh, John," she begged. "It hurts worse."

"She couldn't even get dressed this morning," Nettie interjected. "As it is, she's not wearing a—"

"Nettie!"

"Well, you're not. I don't see what's so shameful about…"

"I'm s'prised y'er even up and movin' around," Billy interrupted. He laid the last strip of bacon on Constance's already loaded plate.

Nettie calmly reached over and snagged it for herself. "I had to milk the cow, too. And carry the pail all the way back, as Cissy can't bend over, not even a little bit."

Constance laid down her biscuit. "I am proud of you, Nettie. You have been a real help." As she spoke she surreptitiously lifted the bacon strip off Nettie's plate and bit into it.

John blinked. "You think you could drive the wagon today, Nettie?"

Nettie looked horrified. "You mean, the oxen? Oh, I don't see how—"

"Sure you can, Nettie girl." Billy wiped the last of the bacon grease from the skillet. "You're plenty smart. Why, I betcha I can learn you how to drive a team in half an hour."

"Teach me," Nettie corrected with a sniff. "*Teach* me how to drive."

"At yer service, ma'am. Now, who's gonna help me with the washin' up here?"

Nettie's lower lip came out. "Oh, all right, I suppose I will have to," she grumbled.

Billy sent the major a covert thumbs-up and Constance ducked her head to hide a smile. Poor Nettie. She really had to pitch in, since Constance was not able to use her arm.

Poor Nettie, indeed! an inner voice countered. As soon as they reached the fort, "Poor Nettie" would marry the major and knowingly break her sister's heart.

John downed the dregs of his coffee. "Let's hitch up and get rolling. We've got another mountain and the north fork of the Platte ahead of us. We're due at Fort Laramie in six days."

Chapter Twenty-One

Over the next two days, the wagon train lumbered up and down three more long hills. Nettie managed to drive the ox team with her jaw set and her arms stiff with tension.

"Told ya so," Billy chortled to the major for the tenth time that morning. He twisted in the saddle to make sure they were out of hearing distance. "Gonna make a growed-up woman outta her yet. Can't stand seein' Miss Constance work so hard and make excuses for her all the time. My momma done the same thing for my pap, until it finally kilt her."

John rode in silence at Billy's side. Two long, arduous days had passed since he'd taken that arrow out of Constance's shoulder. She had surprised him by getting up and dressed the next morning, and now she astounded him by walking beside the blue

Conestoga in Nettie's place, keeping track of the Ramsey brood. He noticed she was a bit unsteady on her feet; probably the moccasins she now wore instead of her high-laced walking shoes. He imagined she'd feel every rock and rut on the trail. She cradled her slinged arm as if it hurt. He'd check the dressing tonight.

The wagon train rolled around a bend and came to a complete stop at the sight of the North Platte River.

The South Platte had been a wide, shallow splash of lazy water one could simply walk across. The North Platte was a different story. Before them a swift black-green river rushed on its way over boulders and around trees with barely a ripple.

"Never seen it so high," Billy remarked. "And no ferry fer a hundred miles."

"We'll float the wagons across," John said.

"Hitched up?"

John hesitated. "Duquette won't like it," he acknowledged. "But there's no other way."

Billy spit off to one side. "I figger Duquette's damn lucky he's got us to think for him. Pretty plain he doesn't know nothin' about travelin'."

"Man doesn't like to look like a fool, Billy. Even if he is one."

Billy snorted. "I seed that right off, Major. No

experience and no horse sense. Fella like him shoulda never left home.''

John rode up and down the riverbank, looking for a level place to enter the swift-flowing current. When he found a spot that shelved off gradually, he signaled Billy.

Predictably, Joshua Duquette objected to the plan, and once again John and the florid-faced wagon master walked off to one side of the trail to parley.

Billy ignored them and spent the time lining up the wagons and reassuring the drivers. ''Major's crossed this here river a hundred times. Just do what he says.''

John returned, his mouth thinned with annoyance, and surveyed the organization Billy had undertaken. ''Don't know how much more of Duquette I can stomach,'' he murmured.

''We goin' across 'r not?''

''Yep. Swim the cow and the horses across first. The oxen will follow if they see another animal swimming ahead of them.''

''Kinda like some people,'' Billy grumbled.

''Duquette's convinced. He doesn't have the balls for another hundred miles to search out a ferry.''

''Only sensible thing to do,'' Billy offered. ''Seed that right off, too. What about them children, John? You want them in the wagons?''

"Nope. We'll take them across on horseback, two at a time. I'll bring Miss Constance across last. I don't want her in the wagon. If anything happens, she won't be able to swim with only one arm. We'll take our nooning on the other side."

"Right," Billy assented. He stepped his horse toward the cluster of children around Constance. "Parker, Elijah, climb right up in front of me here. Ol' Billy's gonna give y'all a ride you ain't never gonna ferget."

John dismounted and lifted the twins, Ruth and Essie, onto his saddle, then remounted and stepped his mare into the water. The girls were quiet as the water lapped at their ankles and then their knees; he wrapped one arm around the two of them and the horse struck out swimming. The Ollesens' horses and the milk cow followed.

Billy and the major reached the opposite bank, unloaded the children and started back to guide the wagons. The first team to stumble down the rocky bank and enter the river was Joshua Duquette's. Once the oxen started to swim, the wagon bobbed along behind them, hauled safely through the current by Billy and the major on horseback using ropes tied to the front axles.

The blue Conestoga was next in line. A white-faced Nettie sat in the driver's seat, and as the team hit the water, she scrunched her eyes shut and began to whimper.

"Oh, I can't do this, I can't! I'm going to drown, I just know I am."

When the oxen began to swim and the dark water lapped at her moccasined feet, she let out a squeal of alarm. "I'm going under! Do something, I'm drown—"

Billy snorted. "Hush up, girl. You ain't drownin', just scared skittish. Now you keep them blue eyes of yourn open and pay attention!"

Nettie's lids snapped up. "You mind your own business, you big bully!" She had to shout over the roar of the river.

"This *is* my business," Billy yelled back. "You listen up, Princess. Watch your team, so it don't head downstream with the current. Whip 'em if ya hafta."

Nettie shot him a venomous look, but she managed a weak snap of her whip over the heads of the animals. She clenched the reins with a white-knuckled grip as the wagon listed sideways and then began to float.

After three hours of grueling work, only nine-year-old Jamie Ramsey and Constance remained on the far bank. While Billy helped Jamie scramble up behind him, John rode up to Constance and dismounted. River water streamed off the mare's flanks, and he himself was soaking wet up to his belt buckle.

"I'll have to put you on my lap since you can't hang on from behind." He positioned his hands at her waist and lifted her onto the saddle. Then he remounted and settled her onto his lap. "Sorry I'm wet," he said.

"It feels good. Cool."

He guided the horse down the now-slippery bank. "You feel…" He didn't finish the thought. She was more than just warm; she was burning up.

"When was your dressing last changed?"

"Yesterday morning. Nettie didn't have time to—"

John swore under his breath. "You should have told me. I'll look at it once we get across."

The horse struck out with its forelegs, and the smooth motion told her the tired animal was swimming. Water soaked her skirt, her petticoat, even her underdrawers.

John patted the mare's neck. "This is the last load, girl. Just a dozen more yards and then…"

"John, we're drifting downriver."

"A bit, yes. Just hold on." He tightened his left arm across her midsection, careful not to jostle her shoulder.

She leaned into him, rested her forehead against his neck.

Her skin was hot. Sticky. His heart constricted. *By God she wasn't going to survive a Sioux arrow three inches from her heart only to die of infection. He wouldn't let her.*

He gripped the horse with his knees and dipped one hand into the water, then smoothed his fingers over her cheeks.

"Cool," she murmured.

He did it again, this time letting the excess water run down her neck and throat. She grasped his wet hand and pressed it where her unbuttoned blouse exposed the skin.

"Don't stop."

He scooped more water, let the horse drift farther downstream. "I haven't had a word with you in private for two days."

"Nettie maneuvers things so you and I are never alone."

"Because?"

"She's frightened. She's afraid you won't marry her."

She felt his arm jerk. "I'll marry her," he growled. "I said I would. I'll get court-martialed if I don't."

"Oh, John, let's don't talk about it."

"I've got to know, Constance. Can you live with it? The way things will be?"

"I can," she said in a choked voice. "If you can."

They were mid-river now, the current pulling them past the wagons assembled on the opposite bank. For a fleeting moment she didn't care. She just wanted to drift with his strong arms around her, his warm breath at her temple. His skin smelled of wood smoke and leather and sweat.

She could not bring herself to think about never being close to him again after he and Nettie were married.

"I'll head back to Fort Kearny right after the wedding," he said. "I can't be near you and not—"

She burrowed her face into his shoulder. "John, I want you to…to promise me something." Her words came out muffled and hesitant.

"Anything. Name it."

"I want to be with you, for us to be together, before you and Nettie…can you arrange that?"

He grazed the top of her head with his lips. "Oh, God, as if I haven't thought of it a thousand times. You don't know how much I want to kiss you, Constance. I'm letting the horse go with the current until we're out of sight and I can."

"And?"

Silence.

"And?" she repeated. She had to remind herself to breathe.

"And the rest, too," he said, his voice quiet. "But first we have to fight this infection. You're running a fever."

They were out of sight now. John guided the mare toward the bank and halted the animal when it got all four hooves onto the narrow beach. He looped the reins around the pommel, then trailed his wet, warm fingers over her face, behind her ear, down her throat to the first pearl button.

"John." She pressed her lips into his palm and felt his body tense.

"I love you, Constance. I want to be with you, even if it can only be that one time."

"We have three days before we reach Fort Laramie."

With his left hand he tipped her chin up. "I'll think of something."

His mouth was salty and warm. She strained toward him, despite the bite of pain in her shoulder, let him open her mouth with his smooth tongue and then withdraw and flick it over her lips. A sweet pain lodged in her groin as she clung to him.

"We've got to stop," he whispered. "But God

forgive me, I don't want to.'' His body trembled against hers.

At last he released her with a groan and took up the reins. He turned the horse back toward the wagon train.

Chapter Twenty-Two

In the privacy of the blue Conestoga, John pushed aside the homespun blouse Constance unbuttoned and inspected the wounds in her shoulder. The entry wound in her back was red and puffy, the surrounding skin swollen and hot to the touch.

Infected. Dammit to hell, why couldn't Nettie at least have *looked* at it?

He clamped his jaw shut. He knew why. Nettie was concerned about herself, not her sister. Maybe with an unborn child she was entitled to turn inward, but a more useless woman he had never encountered.

Constance was shivering. Not from cold, he knew, but from the fever that burned inside her.

"Keep warm," he said shortly. "And don't move around. I'm going to talk to Duquette." He left her curled up on the pallet where she and Nettie slept at night and went to find the wagon master.

The train had halted for their nooning in an expanse of tickle-grass surrounded by three sprawling oaks and the willows growing along the bank of the North Platte. Smoke drifted from cook fires. The Ramsey baby's cries faded as he strode past their dilapidated wagon to the head of the line where Joshua Duquette sat spaddle-legged under an oak tree. His plump, silent wife moved from cook fire to the pantry end of their wagon and back again.

The wagon master's mouth turned down when he saw John approach. "Can't a man eat in peace? What is it now, Major?"

"Constance Weldon is down with fever."

Duquette spit out a mouthful of tea. "So?"

"I suggest we camp here overnight so I can treat her."

"How ya gonna do that, soldier-boy?"

John looked the man in the eye. "Drain the pus from the wound and then sweat the fever out of her."

The wagon master looked past John, focusing on the purple hills to the west. "How long'll all that take?"

"Six, maybe eight hours."

"She gonna die?"

"She will if she doesn't get help."

Duquette grinned as if secretly pleased at something. "Well, now, I tell ya, Major. I'm sick and tired of takin' orders from you. Oh, sure, you always talk things over, man to man, but in the end it's allus your way. Makes me look like I don't know what I'm doin' and I've had about enough."

John said nothing.

Duquette lumbered to an upright position and stood, feet apart, his breath wheezing in and out. "You wanna halt my wagon train an extra day while you doctor a woman careless enough to get an arrow in the back? Over my dead body."

Without warning, he plunged his ham-sized fist into John's stomach, doubling him over. "You're gonna have to lick me first, soldier-boy."

As he spoke, the wagon master peeled off his dirty plaid shirt and yanked it free of his belt while John gasped for breath, his hands on his knees.

Ain't gonna be pretty, Billy had said.

So be it. He knew Duquette was waiting for him to straighten up so he could wallop him again. He spent a few extra precious seconds planning his strategy against a man who outweighed him by thirty pounds.

Surprise, that was it. He lunged at Duquette's knees, taking him down with a gutteral roar.

And all the Cheyenne tricks he could remember.
He scrambled on top of the wagon master and
slanted the edge of his hand into the man's throat.

Not hard enough. Duquette made a choking noise,
but upended John by rolling over. Pinned beneath
the hulk, he hunched into himself and waited. When
the wagon master's body lifted slightly, John drove
his elbow into the man's balls.

Duquette squawked and flailed after John, but he
was too quick. He was on his feet, waiting, when
Duquette staggered upright. The wagon master lowered his head and came at him like a battering ram.
This time, John was ready.

He doubled his fists, clasped them together and
swung back to gather all the momentum possible.
Then he pounded his knuckles into Duquette's jaw.

He kept coming. John stepped out of his path, and
the man crashed onto the ground and lay still.

"Out colder'n a dead moose," a voice said.

John shook his head to clear the cobwebs. True
enough, Joshua Duquette sprawled unconscious at
his feet.

"Better get Eliza," John managed. "And Billy,
bring a bucket of cold water."

"Fer him? Let him get his own—"

"For me," John said, his voice tight. "I think my
hand's broken."

Billy's jaw snapped shut. "Now why'dja do a dumb thing like that, Major? You got to tend Miss Constance."

"Go tell the others we'll camp here. Tell the women they can make it a wash day, since the river's nearby."

"What you gonna do 'bout Miss Constance?"

"Build a sweat lodge. There's willow growing along the bank. I'll need some sage branches and some rocks to heat."

"Shore thing, Major. Anythin' else?"

John thought for a long minute. "Tell Nettie she'll be needed."

"Oh, boy," Billy muttered. "Now there's a scary thought. Oh-boy-oh-boy-oh-boy."

Despite John's painful left hand, with Billy's help he constructed the sweat lodge within an hour, dug the fire pit and filled it with stones and fashioned a soft bed of willow branches inside. The Ramsey children scoured the prairie for sage, laying it in a heap within reach in one corner of the lodge. When everything was ready, John went to the wagon for Constance.

"My head aches," she murmured as he lifted her into his arms. Her teeth chattered with the chills that shook her body. "Cold," she said.

"Not for long." He carried her away from the wagon circle to the sweat lodge, where Billy waited with Nettie.

"Rocks are red-hot, Major. Just tell me when."

"Nettie, you know what to do?"

"I—I'm not sure."

"When Billy pours the water, the steam will rise inside the lodge. Keep your sister quiet and rub her skin with the sage branches to bring out the poison."

"No," Nettie announced. "I can't. It will be so awful hot in there. I cannot abide feeling overheated."

"Oh, fer cryin' out—"

"Never mind," John ordered. He crawled inside the lodge, laid Constance on the willow pallet, then backed out and stood up.

"Billy, bring the water." He began to unbuckle his belt.

Nettie gazed at him, one hand at her mouth. "Why, Major, whatever are you doing?"

"Undressing."

"You can't mean—you're not going to be inside with her... without any clothes..."

"You can take my place," John offered. "One of us has to be with her, she's half out of her head with fever."

"But...but you're a man!"

"Damn right. It's you or me, Nettie. Your sister's life hangs in the balance."

"You do it," she blurted. "I just can't. Besides, you know what to do, and I…"

John shed his shirt and trousers. By the time he got to his underdrawers and his boots, Nettie had fled. He crawled inside and began wrestling Constance out of her clothes. Blouse, skirt, petticoat, underpetticoat, camisole, drawers. He tried not to notice how soft and warm the garments were, tried not to inhale the subtle scent of vanilla that clung to her skin.

And then when she was naked beside him, he tried not to notice how beautiful she was.

He rolled the garments he'd removed into a bundle, taking his time with the task to keep his hands occupied. Constance lay so close to him he could feel the heat from her body, smell the lemony scent of her hair. By the time Billy poured the first dipperful of water over the heated stones in the fire pit at their feet, John had to clench his fingers to keep from touching her.

Her eyes looked glazed. Unfocused. *She's crazed with fever,* he reminded himself. A man did not touch a woman in that condition except as a healer.

"Constance?"

"...he likes walnut cake, Nettie. I'll teach you..."

"Constance, can you hear me?"

"So cold...wrap me up in the quilt, Mama."

More water hissed onto the rocks and steam swirled to fill the blanket-covered lodge. Constance clawed at her shoulder bandage, but John pinned her hand in his so she wouldn't pull out the stitches. At the infection site near her spine, he'd slit open the sutures and drained the wound, then packed it with tree moss. He'd left it open except for a light covering of sterile folded muslin, already limp from the steam.

"It's all dark," she said suddenly. "Why is it so dark?"

"It's night," John said quietly. "If we were outside, we'd see the stars in the sky."

"Stars," she echoed. "Big stars. Little stars. Mama's up there now, in heaven. So sorry for Papa."

John found the stash of sage, lifted a branch and stripped off the leaves. He started at her neck, rubbing the aromatic herb over her skin. The pungent scent made his eyes smart. He closed his lids and kept working the oil into her skin, guided by touch alone.

He tried not to be too conscious of what he was

doing. Instead he imagined he was smoothing his fingers over an injured bird or a sick colt. *Don't think, Johnny. Just do it.*

It was what Father had said when John had to walk to Dr. Barden's with a broken leg. *Don't think.*

And don't feel.

He grabbed another handful of sage leaves.

He dozed off and on, waking when Billy dumped a fresh dipper of water over the hot stones. Gradually Constance grew quieter, her murmurings less and less coherent. The chills had stopped, but her skin was burning.

The air inside the lodge was thick and wet, scented with sage and the salt of his sweat. He worked the crushed sage leaves over her hot, dry skin and waited for the fever to break.

For hours he listened to her shallow, irregular breathing, punctuated by the hiss of water spitting against hot stone. He was losing her. He'd done everything in his power, and she was dying anyway.

Out on the prairie somewhere a coyote howled. For some reason, he thought of Yellow Wolf.

Near dawn, she began to sweat. Perspiration poured off her, slicking her skin, wetting the loose tendrils of hair around her face. Her chest rose and fell in an even rhythm.

John felt for her pulse. Then he brushed his mouth against her forehead. Her skin felt cool.

Thank you, Lord. Thank you.

He laid his head on her breast and gave thanks for the first time since Three Horse Creek.

Chapter Twenty-Three

For two days, Flora Stryker spooned boiled sugar water past Constance's lips as she lay in the jolting wagon recovering from her fever. For the first twenty-four hours, she was so weak she couldn't hold her head up, but with rest and Flora's bean soup, she rapidly regained her strength. John checked her dressings three times each day, murmuring approval over the moss-packed wound in her back, which was healing cleanly. She could even move her right arm without too much pain.

Just a day out of Fox Flat, she surprised everyone, even herself, by getting dressed by herself at dawn and helping Billy prepare breakfast.

"Land's sakes," Flora exclaimed when she came to tend her. "You must be held together by spit and a bit of corset wire."

"No corset," Constance assured her. "I can't lace it. And anyway, I gave it up before we reached Fort Kearny."

"You got sand, all right," Billy said, watching her stir milk into the pancake batter with a wooden spoon held awkwardly in her left hand. "'Nuff to get ya to Oregon and then some." He sent her a sly look. "Now maybe the major'll get some sleep."

"Do you think…" She bent her head over the mixing bowl.

"Not if I can help it," Billy quipped. "What's on yer mind?"

Her stirring hand slowed, then stopped. "Do you think I…we—Nettie and me—are doing the right thing?"

Billy spit on the fire-heated iron griddle. The bit of moisture bubbled into steam. "Hell, no, I don't. Major's marryin' the wrong gal." He lifted the bowl out of her grasp, sloshed the spoon twice around the edge and poured a dollop onto the griddle.

"That don't mean he has much of a choice, seein' how Colonel Butterbrain's got him hog-tied with a court-martial."

He handed the bowl of batter back to her. "Keep stirrin'. Seems a mite too thick. Now, you take yer ever'day army officer, he'll wiggle outta his duty ev'ry chance he gets. John's not like that. The major does what he sets out to do. In this case, what he's *ordered* to do. See, his daddy was an army colonel, 'fore he got shot off his horse in the Mexican War. Major's got some idea his pa's up there in heaven expecting him to do the same.''

"But Billy, I don't want him to get shot off his horse, speaking figuratively, of course." She stirred as fast as she could left-handed. "I just want him to be happy."

"Beggin' yer pardon, Constance, but we both know he ain't gonna be happy with that sister of yours. He ain't gonna stay with her, neither. He's not givin' her his name so's he can be happy—it's the baby he's thinkin' of.''

She handed the bowl back to him.

"He tell ya 'bout Three Horse Creek yet?"

"N-no. Is it important?"

Billy flipped two pancakes with a tin spatula. "Maybe not. It'll decide him whether to stick it out and accept the next promotion, like his pa, or muster out and come west to find you."

He added two more golden-brown cakes to the stack on the speckled tin plate. "Take these on out to the major, now. Jes' put a blob of butter on top. He don't care fer syrup."

"Where will I find him?"

"Aw, he—heck, I don't 'xactly know. Down to

the corral maybe. Young Cal Ollesen had a thing he
wanted to talk over.''

''A 'thing'?''

'''Bout horse breedin'. Cal wants a spotted pony
like mine.''

Constance stopped short at the edge of camp. *A
spotted pony.* It reminded her what this whole journey was about—to build a new life. *Just get there,*
Papa had said. *Think of the future, not the present.*

The future. Cal Ollesen and his brother Arvo
would be successful horse ranchers in Oregon someday. The Nylands, both teachers, would open a
schoolhouse. Friedrich Stryker and his wife, Flora,
who had been a nurse in Missouri, would start a
clinic.

And she and Nettie…

Nettie would bear a child in December, would
care for it, raise it in the clear air of an Oregon
homestead. She herself would live nearby, perhaps
on an adjacent homestead. She'd heard women as
well as men could file claims. Maybe it would all
work out as Papa had planned.

Except for the ache in her heart and soul for the
man her sister would claim as her husband.

She covered the tin plate with a clean napkin and
lifted her chin. Her heart might break, but she could

still walk and talk and hoe corn and make jam and even build a house if she had to.

But she would never marry. Not while Major John Montgomery walked on this earth could she bear to belong to another man.

She swallowed over a tight throat. And besides, in two days, he would belong to Nettie. Even if he never saw her again, John would still be Nettie's husband. Not hers.

The afternoon of their arrival at Fort Laramie was hot and muggy under a cloud-flecked sky. A buttermilk sky, Billy called it. "No rain, jes' teasin.'"

Before the wagons set up camp outside the compound, Nettie sped off in search of the preacher Colonel Butterworth had promised would be there. At supper that evening, they gathered in a silent circle and ate the meal Billy and Constance had cooked—venison steaks and fried tomatoes from the commanding officer's kitchen garden.

No one said a word until their plates were almost empty. Then Nettie, her cheeks flushed, blurted out a short phrase. "Day after tomorrow."

"Fer what?" Billy spoke over a mouthful of meat.

"For the wedding," she reminded. Her blue eyes were shiny and her attention kept shifting from the fire to the wagon. She shifted closer to the major. "*Our* wedding."

Constance's fork clunked onto the plate of food in her lap. John's head came up and their gazes met, his blue eyes steady.

Nettie's voice rose shrilly. "You haven't forgotten we're to be married, have you, Major?"

"I haven't forgotten."

His eyes still held hers. In their depths Constance saw pain and hunger. And resignation. A wave of longing tore through her, sharper than any scalpel cut or arrow ripping her flesh. She shut her eyes. She would gladly trade that agony for this. At least the pain of an arrow would end.

She set her plate on the blanket beside her and watched, her mind and body numb, as John rose and walked off into the dark.

"There he goes again," Nettie complained. "I don't know why he needs to go off by himself all the time." She giggled. "You'd think he had a guilty secret!"

Dumbfounded, Constance stared at her sister. At that moment she hated the golden curls, the syrupy voice, yes, even the child she carried in her womb.

"Sister?" Her voice trembled with fury. "It is time you grew up. Do not—ever—treat a man's private thoughts or the burdens he carries on his shoulders with disrespect or as a source of amusement. Do you hear me, Nettie? If you are to be married in two days' time, you had better start practicing now on the things that make a wife out of a shallow, thoughtless, self-centered little girl.''

"And I suppose you know all about how to be a wife? I'm not so shallow, Cissy."

Constance just looked at her.

"Well, I'm not," Nettie wailed. "I can embroider and play the piano and…and even drive an ox team. So there!''

Billy rose, helped Nettie to her feet and pulled her toward the cook fire. "And y'er the best durn dishwasher west of the Missippi. Come on, little g— Miss Nettie. I'll help you with the dryin'.''

Constance sat staring into the fire until her vision blurred. She was vaguely aware of Billy lifting her plate off the blanket, the clatter of spoons against the tin dishpan, Billy's raspy voice answering Nettie's lighter one.

Nettie stacked the dirty plates into a pile. "What did I say that was so wrong?"

Constance stood up unsteadily. She didn't want to hear any more. She wanted to be with John, wanted to look up at the stars and feel that the problems down here on this earth were small and unimportant in the grand scheme of the universe.

''Well, ta start with, when it comes to men, missy, you got too much sass and not enough…''

Billy's voice faded as Constance moved away from the firelight toward the open plain and the cover of darkness.

She had never seen the stars so luminous. Against the black curtain of a moonless night, they looked like thousands upon thousands of flickering candles. How huge the universe was. And how small she felt at this moment.

John turned at her approach but said nothing. She walked to him and leaned her forehead against his shoulder.

''I am beginning to hate my own sister,'' she said in a choked voice. Her throat ached, and her head as well. Everything ached, except—oddly—the arrow wounds in her shoulder and her back.

''Because of what she—and I—are doing?''

''No. Because of *how* she is doing it. It's as if she takes pleasure in hurting me. In flaunting her victory.''

''Nettie doesn't understand,'' he said in a low voice.

''Oh, yes she does, John. She knows exactly what she is doing.''

''I mean about relationships. Love. A man and a woman.''

"She's carrying a man's seed. She must understand something."

His breath rasped in. "Not enough. Not what is important."

They stood in silence, listening to the soft chuckle of night birds and the far-off yip-yip of a coyote. She pressed her hands against his chest. His heartbeat thudded under her palms.

When he spoke, his voice was hoarse. "Tomorrow night I'm going to camp by myself, down by the river."

"Why?"

"It's the last chance we'll have to be together."

"You know I will come to you, John. You need not even ask."

He removed her hands from his chest and held them. "I do need to ask. And before you answer, there are things I have to tell you. Things I haven't put into words before a living soul because... because I couldn't face them myself."

"I do not need to hear about Little Star," she murmured. "I know already that you loved her."

"You do not know all of it. Only now, when I no longer feel that I am only half a man, have I the courage the speak of it."

"Then tell me. Tell me what weighs on you, and then ask me again to come to the river."

He waited a long time before he spoke, caressing the back of her neck with his fingers.

"Last fall, October, Colonel Butterworth ordered a raid on a Cheyenne encampment near Three Horse Creek. Seems he'd been losing horses from the post remuda, and he figured it was Indians. Probably was, but not the Cheyenne. At least not those Cheyenne. It was a winter camp, mostly women and children.

"I tried to tell him, but he wouldn't listen. He put me in charge of the detail with orders to locate the camp and bring back the horses.

"Little Star and I had been married since summer. She had left the fort and gone to visit her grandmother, so she was in the camp when the soldiers got there. My men found a few of the horses, not the whole lot, but a few. I gave orders to round them up, but one was picketed outside the chief's tepee, and when the chief objected, some damn fool green corporal shot him.

"It started a bloodletting I'll never forget. A massacre. When I saw I couldn't stop it, I went to find Little Star.

"Someone threw a firebrand onto the tepee, and when Little Star and her grandmother came out…"

He stopped. Waited until he could go on.

"The old woman died right away. But Little

Star…'' Again he swallowed, struggling to continue.

"She was hit once in the belly and once in the chest. She was still alive when I got to her, but the pain must have been awful. I remember she reached up to me and said, 'Please, John.' And when I drew my revolver, she smiled, and I knew what she wanted. I put it to her temple.

"I—I killed her. She was dying anyway, and I pulled the trigger to make it easier."

Deep inside, her heart twisted in agony. "You gave her a great gift, John. Peace."

"But she was my wife. I loved her. As long as I live I won't be able to forget that."

"And that is what is between you and Yellow Wolf," she said.

"Yellow Wolf was her brother. And a coward. He killed the corporal and then turned on me. When he ran from the camp, I shot him and missed. My bullet caught him in the elbow."

"What you must do, John, is forgive yourself. You need not forget it, any of it. Yes, you took her life, but it was done in love."

"Until this moment, until I spoke these words out loud to you, I had not thought it possible to live and be whole again."

"I am beginning to believe that anything is possible."

"Tomorrow night, Constance. Will you come?"

Her answer came low and steady. "I will come."

Chapter Twenty-Four

My hand shakes so violently I fear I cannot write, and yet I must. Anguish washes over me, making the hurt in my shoulder a small matter indeed. If I am to live through this awful longing, and the lonely time I see ahead, I must release my feelings in some way. To this end, my journal must suffice.

John has told me of Three Horse Creek and how his wife died; it made my whole insides scream for the pain in his voice. He is a man who can love beyond himself, and I cannot help but think that God, if there is someone watching over us, will not cause him to suffer further.

As for me, I tell myself over and over again that I am brave and strong, but in the next minute I know it is a lie. I do not want John to marry Nettie. She will hurt him and he deserves better.

I try to think of the future, of when we will finally get to Oregon. Nettie's life, and that of her child, are just beginning; mine, I fear, is ending here on these godforsaken plains.

Except that I will have my hour in John's arms. At this moment, that is all that matters.

Constance unfolded the ivory lace gown and shook out the lavender blossoms her mother always used to scent her garments. On impulse she buried her nose in the delicate fabric and inhaled deeply. The familiar spicy fragrance brought tears to her eyes. *Oh, Mama, how I miss you. It's been so hard without you.*

"Is that it, Cissy?" Nettie reached both hands for the dress. "However did you manage to save it?"

"John saved it. He emptied the drawers in the chiffonier we had to unload and stored the things in the Ollesens' wagon."

"Give it to me."

Constance stepped back from her sister's grasping fingers. Mama's wedding dress was precious to her; it was the last tangible link with her mother. It meant nothing to Nettie, who had never known any mother but Constance. Her childhood had ended with Nettie's birth.

"Perhaps that is where it went wrong," she murmured.

"Where what went wrong? Cissy, are you going to give me that dress or not?" Nettie's voice was unusually strident this evening, and Constance clamped her lips tight shut. Her sister should be happy on the eve of her marriage.

"Yes, Sister, I will give you the dress. I was just…saying goodbye to it."

"Goodbye to your hopes, you mean?"

Constance felt the sting of her words as keenly as if Nettie had struck her. "Why, Nettie, what a cruel thing to say!" She blinked back tears that stung under her lids.

"Well, hurry up and give me the dress, then. The wedding is tomorrow at noon. I have to try it on, check the length, then check the…waist. You might have to move the buttons over."

Constance stared up at the canvas ceiling over her head, counted to twenty and then looked at Nettie, sitting cross-legged on their sleeping pallet. *Lord, forgive me, but I long to slap her right across the face, even if she is my sister.*

She fought to keep her voice even. "Nettie, you will have to move the buttons yourself. And fix the hem. And press out the fold lines. I am going to bed."

"But...but you can't, Cissy!" Her voice quavered with the false distress Constance had come to recognize. "I'm getting married tomorrow!"

"I will be here for you tomorrow." She swallowed hard and handed the soft lace gown to her sister. "But tonight is my own. And I do not wish to spend it here in this wagon, working for you."

"Oh, go on then." Nettie flung the words at her in an injured tone. "Who wants you, anyway?" Her voice quavered.

For a moment a spasm of guilt seized her, stopping her in her tracks halfway to the canvas curtain at the front of the wagon. *I can't. I can't leave her, my only sister, when she needs me.*

She closed her fingers around the bonnet lacing and held on tight. *But I must. I must have my own happiness. I must have myself.*

All she had to do was step through the opening, step into the soft summer night and go to John. Tomorrow was the beginning of not only Nettie's new life, but her own. *My sister will marry the man I love, and I will make of it the best that I can. But now, tonight, I must—I will—have something for me.*

"Good night, Nettie. The sewing basket is on the top shelf. And do not call out for me tonight, Sister. I will not hear you."

She moved through the bonnet and put her foot

onto the jockey box. A saddled horse waited near the back of the wagon. Billy's brown and white spotted mare.

Two miles to the south, John had said. She lifted the animal's reins, put her foot in the stirrup and grasped the pommel with her left hand. Then she paused to look up at the stars in the night sky.

What I am doing is for me.

And for John.

She flicked the reins and walked the mare away from camp, away from Nettie, toward the river.

She did not look back.

When she came to the river, she followed the flicker of a campfire to the east. She knew it was John; the horse seemed to know the way. She guessed the major and Billy had camped here before, perhaps while guiding another wagon train. Billy, bless his rambunctious soul, was no doubt asleep under the wagon at this hour, looking out for Nettie.

But even if he weren't, she knew she would be doing just what she was—riding out to find John and be with him for this one night. The most important night of her life.

Everything seemed unreal. In her wildest dreams

she never imagined doing such a thing, leaving Nettie on her own and...and...

She drew in a deep lungful of the sweet night air. And giving herself to a man. She wanted it—him— more than anything on this earth. She wanted it to be beautiful.

John heard the horse, the slow, steady hoofbeats on the grass he'd trampled not three hours earlier, and he rose from where he sat by the fire. When she reached the circle of firelight he moved toward her.

She slid off the mare into his arms, and he felt the slight tremor of her frame along with the throb of her heartbeat against his chest. He stood with his arms around her for some minutes, saying nothing.

Part of him could not believe she was here with him. Another part of him knew that she was safe in his arms at this moment and it was the last time she would ever be so. Tomorrow, after the ceremony, he'd head back to Fort Kearny and tell the colonel what a damn fool he was. That alone would probably get him court-martialed.

He put his mouth near her ear. "Yellow Wolf tells me I don't deserve you."

"Yellow Wolf does not know everything we know, John. He is angry at himself because he showed his cowardice. I am angry at myself for the same failing.''

''You are the bravest woman I have ever known,'' he whispered.

''I am also a coward. From the very beginning, when Nettie was born and Mama died, I have been a coward. It is—was—harder to stand up for myself, to ask for what I needed, than it was to cater to what my sister needed. I let what *she* wanted be more important than anything else.''

''What did you want?'' He began kissing her temple, her closed eyelids.

''I wanted...I want to love a man. A good man, who loves me back. Who wants a home. Children.''

''You have such a man,'' he said, his voice quiet. ''I want, or wanted, all those things. A child, especially.'' His lips found her mouth. She tasted of salt and the sweet, ripe peaches Billy had scrounged for their supper. Her heart fluttered like a caged bird under his hand.

He wanted her so bad he didn't think he could stand it much longer. He needed to touch her. Needed her to put her hands on him, against his naked skin. On his sex.

''The Cheyenne say all things come when the time is right.''

She lifted her head. ''We will not have a child,

John. My courses will come in two days' time. But we will have each other for this one night, and that is enough.''

"The hell it is.''

She moved her hand to the neck of her blouse and began to unbutton it. "Do not talk, John. We are wasting time.''

She lifted his hand, placed his fingers against her exposed throat. "Undress me.''

He worked the buttons quietly, methodically, feeling the heat from her breasts as he separated the garment and worked it off her shoulders. She made a little moan of pleasure and arched her body toward him, offering herself.

John bent his head, found the soft nipple under the muslin camisole, warmed it with his breath and began circling it with his wet tongue.

"Yes,'' she whispered. "Now this.'' She drew his hands to her waist. "Undo my skirt.''

Without moving his mouth from her breast, he reached around her and undid the fastening. She stepped forward, and the blue muslin dropped over her hips. Quickly he unknotted the ties of her petticoat and then her underdrawers. His breathing grew uneven. *Lord, she has no idea what she is doing to me.*

He moved to her other breast. She raised her arms

over her head and shimmied out of her lower undergarments while he untied the ribbon of her camisole, lifted it over her head. Her hands dropped to his belt buckle.

He felt the tug as her fingers worked the metal tongue free, felt her warm hands circle the bare skin at his waist.

"I don't wear drawers," he murmured.

"Good." She slipped both hands under the straining denim and suddenly he couldn't take any more.

"Constance." His voice was gravelly. "Stop before I—"

"Take off your shirt, John. And your trousers. Take off…everything."

She stood apart from him and watched while he shucked his boots and socks and stepped out of his pants. He was shaking so much he had trouble unlacing his shirt and pulling it off. He tossed it away, but she snatched it up before it landed and buried her face in it.

"It smells just like you," came her muffled voice.

Then she raised her head and looked at him. Looked at his chest, the scar across his left shoulder, his face, his belly, his sex, his face again.

"I have never seen a man before," she breathed. "You are beautiful. Wanting you makes my knees feel funny."

He picked her up in his arms, weak with relief. She saw him not as the wounded shell of a man he'd been for so long, but whole. Vital. When he settled her onto his bedroll before the fire, she clung to him with unexpected strength in both arms.

"Does it hurt you to move?" he asked.

She shook her head, traced her fingers down the side of his face, then across the raised flesh on his chest.

"It's a lance wound," he said. "Yellow Wolf missed my heart, but made his mark on me just the same."

"Don't think of it. Think about being alive. About being here with me." She pulled his head down and he kissed her slowly. Deeply.

Constance felt his firm lips move on hers, his tongue touch the inside of her mouth. His hand lay between them, and he moved it downward until it rested between her thighs.

He stroked her gently, deliberately, using his thumb and forefinger to open her feminine folds and enter. She moved against him but he held her hips still, his hand shaking. He touched her inner lips, murmured a word, then began to lick her nipples.

She felt hot and languid with the sweet pleasure that swept through her. *So this was love. It was so simple. So beautiful.*

She smoothed her palms over his belly and heard his breath catch. She moved lower, touching him with the tips of her fingers and his body went completely still.

"Constance," he said against her mouth. "Don't stop."

Again his hand found her opening, dipped inside and spread the moisture over her throbbing flesh. The feel of his fingers moving, stroking, was so exquisite it was almost unbearable. She spread her legs.

He rose over her, pressed the tip of his member at her entrance and pushed forward. He withdrew, then entered her again, going deeper. Each time he repeated the motion, she took a little more of him. It felt…as if she were filling up with something warm and solid inside her.

"Are you all right?" he whispered. "Tell me. I'm trying to go slow."

She let her body answer, arched upward when he thrust again and felt something deep inside her open to him. She slid her hands to his buttocks, and he thrust in again, hard and deep.

She cried out with pleasure, cried out again when he sucked her nipple and slid the full length of him inside her. Her inner muscles contracted around him, and he made a low groaning sound.

Delighted, she did it again, and he began to move. Her fingers spread, clenched, spread again as a searing tension coiled inside her. He drove into her again and again, and when her release came she called his name while her body pulsed in waves of ecstasy. Then she held his shuddering frame and wept with the joy and pleasure of carnal joining.

And at that moment she knew she would never be the same.

Chapter Twenty-Five

They rode back toward camp side by side, not talking, while the sun bathed the morning with soft gold light and bees hummed among the tall purple coneflowers. They were so close their knees could almost touch, so attuned to each other they breathed in and out as one being. A mile from camp they reined in their mounts and reached out to each other for one final embrace.

The major's face was strained, his blue eyes carefully expressionless, his mouth twisting. Constance felt his arms tighten about her, his lips settle over hers for a brief, intense moment. Tears spilled from under her closed eyelids.

"Live well," he whispered.

He broke from her, kicked his mare and wheeled away to the south. He would not return to camp for three hours, and then he would arrive from a different direction.

She watched the tall figure ride away from her and fought the wave of longing in her belly. *You are mine,* he had said. *Mine.* He said it again and again during the hours they had been together. She knew why. Possession, belonging to each other in the way they now did, would make it possible for him to leave.

But knowing it did not help. Pain like a white-hot lance split her heart.

She walked the spotted horse into camp, reached the blue Conestoga before anyone was stirring except for the chattering sparrows. Even Billy still slept underneath the wagon, and last night's cook fire was nothing but gray ash.

She dismounted, looped the mare's reins over the hand brake and stirred up the fire. Still-warm coals emerged from beneath the banked ashes. Trying to forget the ache in her throat, she fed them a twist of dry grass and then a quarter-round of wood Billy had split the night before.

Please, Lord, just let me get through this one day.

She lifted her blue muslin apron from its nail at the back of the wagon, tied it on over her work skirt and wiped her eyes with the hem. She must manage somehow to breathe in, breathe out. Walk. Speak.

Eat breakfast without betraying the anguish that tore at her insides.

She would even help Nettie dress for the wedding. She closed her eyes at the insistent pain that flowered in her stomach.

The next thing she knew, Billy stood beside her, scratching his belly. With his sleep-tousled taffy-colored hair and his bare toes peeking from under his trouser legs he didn't look much older than the major.

"Ya see what Yellow Wolf done left for ya?"

"Yellow Wolf?" She'd left three loaves of bread in the crotch of an oak tree the day before they reached Fort Laramie. "Yellow Wolf was here?" She couldn't get her mind to make a connection.

Billy nodded. "Come last night, he did. Listened to my fiddle for a while, but didn't show hisself. I knowed he was there, though. Man smells like a bucket of bear grease."

"Did Nettie—?"

"Aw, heck no. I watched her close. She never put a foot outside that wagon, just sat and sewed till past midnight. Plumb wore my bowing arm out keepin' her entertained."

"You said Yellow Wolf left something?"

Billy's pale blue eyes danced. "Around t'other side of the wagon."

Constance tiptoed past the closed canvas bonnet and peeked around the corner. Tethered to the rear wagon wheel was an elegant little gray pony with black mane and tail.

"Oh, how beautiful! It's a horse, Billy!"

"Sure 'nuf looks like one," Billy said with a grin.

"But…why?"

Billy crawled back under the wagon to find his boots. "Weddin' present." His voice sounded as if he were upside down.

Her heart leaped and then plummeted to her stomach in the space of a second. "It's for Nettie, then. Not me."

"Nope. It's fer you, all right."

"But I'm not m-marrying the major. My sister is."

Billy poked his head out from under the wagon. "You know that, an' I know that. But Yellow Wolf, he don't know that. He left the pony for you."

"But…but…"

"I seed it right off, I did. Now, when the major gets here he kin read the picture writing painted on that animal's hind quarters."

"Just where *is* the major?" a clear voice asked. Nettie stood in the wagon entrance, her face still creased from sleep, her golden hair in disarray.

"He'll be along," Billy replied. He shot Constance a quick look. "Bein' a major an' all, he sleeps at the officers' quarters."

"Cissy, I can't get the hem right on Mama's dress. I need you to pin it up for me."

Billy caught her gaze once more. His clear blue eyes shone with a mixture of sympathy, exasperation and amusement. He propped his hands on his hips, waiting for her reply.

The memory of the night she had spent with John, the wonder of their being together dissolved the knot of anger against Nettie she had held inside her. Nettie would never know John, would never be loved or cherished by him, as she was. Her resentment toward her sister melted.

She climbed into the jockey box and put her arms around Nettie. "After breakfast, pet. You can stand on the flour barrel and I will measure the hem and baste it up."

Throughout the morning, Constance kept herself busy with the milking and making breakfast and helping Nettie stitch the wedding gown. When John finally rode in, he wolfed down six biscuits and two mugs of black coffee without looking at her. He didn't stay long enough to read the pony's markings, but at half past eleven, disappeared somewhere with Billy.

And then all at once the morning had flown by and it was time for the ceremony.

"Oh," Nettie exclaimed, her round blue eyes flashing. "So soon? Oh good. It is all happening just as I planned."

Not soon enough, Constance thought. Every minute of this day was a bittersweet agony. She loved John. She had willingly, joyfully given herself to him. But in an hour's time he would bind himself not to her, but to her sister.

And then he would mount his horse and ride away, out of her life.

She lifted their mother's ivory lace gown and settled it over Nettie's head, arranged the folds of the skirt and buttoned the ruffled cuffs at her wrists. She dressed herself in her yellow muslin. Her heart felt as if it were squeezing smaller and smaller beneath her rib cage.

While Nettie fussed with her unruly blond curls, Constance unbound the thick single braid she wore and brushed her hair left-handed until her arm tingled. She looked up to find Nettie staring at her.

"Cissy, do you hate me for marrying the major?"

Her brushing arm dropped to her side. "My heart hurts, yes. But I do not hate you, Nettie. You are my sister. I am distressed and angry, but I do not—"

"You wanted him, didn't you?"

Constance looked straight into her sister's face. "Yes. I did."

"And…and it's too late now. Isn't it?"

She felt sick inside. "You carry a child, Sister. John has offered you, and the baby, his name."

Nettie gave her a slow smile. "Just think, Cissy. All my life I've been your baby sister. Now, in just a few moments I will be a grown-up married woman."

Constance bit the inside of her cheek. "You will be my married sister, yes. The 'grown-up' part may take more than just reciting your vows."

"Do you not think life is funny, the way it turns things upside down at times?"

Constance made no reply. Only for the very young and irresponsible could life be considered 'funny.' Life was unexpected. Glorious at times. Heartbreaking.

But not funny.

"It's near noon, Nettie. The major will be waiting."

What am I to do? God forgive me, but for the first time in my life I wish to be free of Nettie. I do not want to be responsible for her. I can scarcely bring myself to look in her face come the morning.

My heart aches. My head pounds as if an ax were

beating at my temples. I can see no way out of this
trap my sister has woven with her lies and her whee-
dling. I am angry, so very angry at her selfishness.
How I wish I could hate her. Oh Papa, Papa, I feel
she has killed us both.

What am I to do? There is nothing. Nothing!

Constance moved past whitewashed clay out-
buildings and two large white frame houses in the
inner compound, feeling as if time had slowed to a
snail's crawl. Never in her entire life had her legs
felt so wooden.

It was a short walk from the wagon across the
parade grounds to the two-story house that served
as officers' quarters. On the lower floor was a large
reception room where the ceremony would be held.

Through the open doorway, she glimpsed rows of
wooden benches and a motley assortment of
straight-backed chairs arranged to make an informal
aisle. At the far end stood a cloth-draped table with
a large black leather-bound Bible resting on top.
Nettie gripped Constance's hand.

Every single seat was occupied, and some of the
soldiers even stood around the perimeter of the
room. The preacher, in an outdated black frock coat,
waited off to one side with a scrubbed and clean-
shaven Billy West. The major stood next to him,

erect and unsmiling in a crisp blue military uniform with multiple stripes of gold braid at the shoulders and on the high collar.

"You go in first, Cissy," Nettie whispered. "You're to stand up with me."

Unable to utter a word over the lump in her throat, she gave her sister's soft hand a final squeeze and stepped into the doorway. At the sight of her, the Ramsey children scurried to their seats and sat in rapt silence.

Constance moved on into the room. She did not dare look at John for fear her feet would refuse to obey her. She looked instead at Billy, took a second step forward, then a third, and started down the aisle.

The wiry army man wore a clean gray military shirt and blue trousers. In one hand he held a dress gray hat she had never seen him wear. In the other he clutched two bouquets of wildflowers, small white roses and purple coneflowers, tied with a white ribbon. When she drew near, he stepped forward and pressed the smaller bunch into her hand.

A soft "aah" rose behind her, and she knew Nettie had entered. Constance turned to watch.

Her sister drifted toward her, graciously acknowledging the smiles and murmurs of approval with a radiant smile. Mrs. Nyland dabbed at her eyes with a lace-edged handkerchief, and Constance felt her own eyes fill with tears.

Ruth Ramsey poked her sister Essie. "*B* is for bee-you-ti-ful," the twins chimed in unison. Laughter rippled among the assembled onlookers.

Nettie gazed straight ahead. When she had almost reached the preacher, Billy again stepped forward and presented her with the wedding bouquet. Someone blew his nose, a man Constance guessed by the drawn-out sound, and at the back of the room someone got the hiccups. One of the Ramsey boys, probably. She smiled in spite of herself.

Life went on, in large ways and small, no matter how one's heart ached.

Nettie stepped up to the preacher and took the major's proffered arm. Billy and Constance positioned themselves on either side of the couple.

I will not think of John, she resolved. *I will think instead of Nettie and her need. Her happiness.*

The preacher opened the thick black book, splayed his manicured fingers across the back of the binding and cleared his throat.

"Dearly beloved…"

Constance's chest constricted. She shut her eyes, forced herself to concentrate.

"…come now before us to be united in holy matrimony."

Nettie moved a step closer to the major, who stood at rigid attention.

"…if there are any among you who know of any impediment…"

Her mind felt light, as if she were outside herself, watching. She saw herself in the yellow muslin dress, standing beside her sister who was wearing Mama's wedding gown. She looked down on Nettie, on John and Billy West, as if she were floating above them.

And in that instant everything became clear.

Impediment? Of course there is an impediment.

It was all wrong. All upside down, as Nettie had said. She had spent so many years catering to her sister's needs and wants she had not recognized the unvarnished truth of her own life until this moment.

I deserve more than this. More than second-best.

"…impediment to this union, let him speak now or forever hold his peace."

A silence as thick as buttermilk fell. One breath in. Out. Two breaths in…

And then three voices broke the stillness at the same time.

"I object."

"I speak out to object."

"By God, I say no."

Chapter Twenty-Six

A hush fell over the wedding guests so profound Constance wondered if she was dreaming. Even the squirming Ramsey children were stunned into silence. The frock-coated preacher stood stock-still, goggling at the bride and groom and their two attendants.

"Beg pardon?"

The quiet stretched on.

Finally the major stepped forward. "I cannot marry this woman in good faith," he said in a low voice. His blue eyes found hers, and within their depths Constance saw both triumph and defeat.

"I cannot because I do not love her. I love her sister, Constance."

Nettie turned to her in astonishment. John looked over Nettie's head and continued in a low voice.

"I tried, Constance. But I have to be honest with myself. I can't take Nettie when it's you I want."

The preacher gripped his Bible with shaking fingers. "What exactly are you saying, Major Montgomery?"

"I am saying," John replied in a voice that carried to the back of the room, "that I cannot marry Henrietta Weldon."

Nettie stared at Constance in wordless accusation. The silence lengthened until Constance could hear her own breath pull in and out, and Nettie's irregular inhalation as well.

Constance took her hand. "Yes, Sister. I am sorry, but I also object." She spoke so softly only Nettie could hear. "I cannot stand by while you take my only happiness. I have done so all my life, and I can no longer. I do love you, Nettie, but it is time that you stand on your own two feet. And it is time for me to reach out for what I want. For what I deserve."

Nettie's face went white. "I—I know it was wrong of me, Cissy," she whispered. "It was selfish and…well, selfish. Truly, I don't want you to be unhappy, I just wanted…" Her blue eyes brimmed with tears.

The preacher harrumphed. "Well. *Well.* I gather that this wedding—" he gestured toward the major and Nettie before him "—is, uh, well...has met an impediment. Yes, that is it. Quite so. And therefore—" He snapped the Bible closed.

"Hold up jes' one minute, Mister preacher." Billy West stepped past the major, lifted Nettie's bouquet out of her grasp and took both her small hands in his.

"I've been watchin' Miss Nettie close up fer some time now. She can surely be a pain in the pincushion an' a real handful, but fer all that I've come to care for her in the deepest way a man can."

Nettie's mouth dropped open.

"My full name's William Martin West. If'n she'll have me, to marry and learn with, she'll never in this life want fer nothin.'

Nettie snapped her mouth shut, then opened it again.

"Anything," she corrected in a soft voice.

While Constance watched in bewilderment, Nettie retrieved her bouquet, stepped to Billy's side and turned toward the preacher.

"Well, I'll be jiggered," the frock-coated man sputtered. "Same ceremony, different couple."

In the next moment Constance found herself gathered into John's arms. "Marry me," he murmured. "Today. Now."

Marry him? Oh, she would die of happiness right

here before the whole assembly! All she could manage was a nod. Her heart singing, she took her place beside him, next to her sister and Billy.

"I see," the preacher muttered, bobbing his head. "I don't believe it, but I do see. First no ceremony. Then a ceremony for a different couple. Then—" he sighed and rolled his eyes toward the ceiling "—a double ceremony." He flipped his Bible open.

"Dearly beloved," he recited rapidly. "If-there-are-any-among-you-who-know-of-any-reason-why-these-two…uh…four should not be joined—"

"Skip that part," the major intoned. He turned to Constance, lifted her hands into his and raised his voice. "I, John Marshall Montgomery, take you, Constance Elizabeth Weldon…"

And so they were married.

When the congratulations and the laughter and the weeping were over, the guests ambling back to wagons and soldiers' quarters, Billy West and John gathered in the center of the reception hall with their new brides on their arms to hold a hurried conference.

Billy spoke first. "We'll take the north camp, Major. If'n that's all right with you, Nettie." He still held her hand, bouquet and all, as if he couldn't yet believe she was his.

Nettie said nothing, just pressed her cheek against his shoulder, smiled and blushed a rosy red.

John tightened his arm about Constance, pulling her close. "We'll ride south for tonight."

Billy dug the toe of his boot into the plank floor. "What about tomorrow, Major? You thought that fer ahead?"

"We'll rendezvous at sunup, ride hard to Fort Kearny and straighten all this out. Then we'll have to ride like prospectors to reach Farewell Bend before the wagon train."

Billy reached his free hand to slap John on the shoulder. "Told ya it'd work out. I seed it right off."

Nettie's soft voice rose. "I *saw* it right off."

Billy just grinned. "Well, I shore did." He smacked a kiss on Nettie's still pink cheek. "I seed it the minute I 'layed' my eyes on you."

John squeezed Constance's arm. "Then it's on to Oregon, all of us together."

"Oh!" Nettie burbled. "Oh, I am so very happy!"

Constance studied her sister's flushed, smiling face, then caught Billy's eye. "We are a family, now," she observed in a quiet voice. "I am glad we are together."

She turned to John, looked up into his steady blue eyes. "For better or worse."

He leaned down to kiss her. "Out here in the West they say, 'Come hell or high water.'"

Epilogue

September 1860

John and Billy arrived in Farewell Bend from Fort Kearny today. They drove up in a flatbed wagon and I could scarcely believe my eyes—not just the sight of them, but in the back of the wagon were the chiffonier and Mama's rose oak sideboard we had left behind at California Hill.

We had some surprises waiting for them, as well. Nettie's waistline pushes her apron out in front until it looks as if she carries a sack of flour underneath her skirt. And I had to confess to John privately that I am feeling woozy in the mornings and often lose my breakfast before noon.

I must go and start supper for the men…and will return later to finish this.

November 1860

The Montgomerys and the Wests have claimed land in Oregon and not only that, have constructed sturdy frame houses within a mile of each other, near the town of Russell's Landing on the Willamette River.

Arvo and Cal Ollesen bought a ranch nearby and have started to breed horses. The Nylands built not one but two split log cabins on a good-sized plot of land just outside town; they will live in one, and the other will serve as a schoolhouse.

Friedrich and Flora Stryker traveled to Portland and purchased a Washington hand press discarded from an army post there. They intend to start a newspaper, *The Willamette Valley Voice.* Joshua and Eliza Duquette have built the Forest Grove Hotel, with a fancy dining room on one side and a saloon on the other. Billy says the whiskey there is awful. John won't set foot in the place.

The Duquettes plan to open a dry goods store within the month.

Clara and Enos Ramsey found a ramshackle two-story farmhouse in the middle of a forty-acre cherry orchard and have settled into farming. Five of their children walk the town road to attend the Nylands' school, and by Christmas, Mrs. Nyland says, all of them, even the four-year-old twins Ruth and Essie,

*will be able to read and recite "Hiawatha" from
memory.*

*Oh, yes, and Mrs. Nyland wants Nettie to tutor at
the school in her spare time. Billy is so proud you'd
think it was him Mrs. Nyland wanted!*

One morning in late December, after a light snow-
fall that covered the trees and meadows with drifts
of white lace, Constance and John Montgomery set
out on horseback for a Christmas visit with her sister
and her husband.

At the door of their trim white house, Billy met
them with a tiny pink bundle in his arms. "Meet
Sage Martin West," he said proudly. "I done
brung...brought...her myself early yesterday mornin'."

Constance flew inside to sit with a beaming Nettie, while John and Billy West walked to the edge
of the front porch.

"You've done well, Billy."

"Aw, it t'weren't, uh...t'wasn't so much. Nettie's
stronger than she knows."

"Constance is, too. Our first will be born next
spring. Mind-boggling, isn't it, how it all worked
out?"

"I told ya so, Major. Jes' listen to ol' Billy now
and again. I seed..."

His words were lost as the two grinning men embraced.

And inside the bedroom of the snug white frame house, Constance and her sister rocked in each other's arms and wept with joy.

Afterword

Sage Martin West, born on December 27, in the year 1860, grew up to turn the town of Russell's Landing upside down.

But that is another story.

* * * * *

*Look for Sage's story coming
soon from Harlequin Historicals.*

Your opinion is important to us! Please take a few moments to share your thoughts with us about your experiences with Harlequin and Silhouette books. Your comments will be very useful in ensuring that we deliver books you love to read. *Please take a few minutes to complete the questionnaire, then send it to us at the address below.*

Send your completed questionnaires to:
Harlequin/Silhouette Reader Survey, P.O. Box 9046, Buffalo, NY 14269-9046

1. As you may know, there are many different lines under the Harlequin and Silhouette brands. Each of the lines is listed below. Please check the box that most represents your reading habit for each line.

Line	Currently read this line	Do not read this line	Not sure if I read this line
Harlequin American Romance	❑	❑	❑
Harlequin Duets	❑	❑	❑
Harlequin Romance	❑	❑	❑
Harlequin Historicals	❑	❑	❑
Harlequin Superromance	❑	❑	❑
Harlequin Intrigue	❑	❑	❑
Harlequin Presents	❑	❑	❑
Harlequin Temptation	❑	❑	❑
Harlequin Blaze	❑	❑	❑
Silhouette Special Edition	❑	❑	❑
Silhouette Romance	❑	❑	❑
Silhouette Intimate Moments	❑	❑	❑
Silhouette Desire	❑	❑	❑

2. Which of the following best describes why you bought *this book?* One answer only, please.

the picture on the cover	❑	the title	❑
the author	❑	the line is one I read often	❑
part of a miniseries	❑	saw an ad in another book	❑
saw an ad in a magazine/newsletter	❑	a friend told me about it	❑
I borrowed/was given this book	❑	other: _____	❑

3. Where did you buy *this book?* One answer only, please.

at Barnes & Noble	❑	at a grocery store	❑
at Waldenbooks	❑	at a drugstore	❑
at Borders	❑	on eHarlequin.com Web site	❑
at another bookstore	❑	from another Web site	❑
at Wal-Mart	❑	Harlequin/Silhouette Reader	❑
at Target	❑	Service/through the mail	
at Kmart	❑	used books from anywhere	❑
at another department store	❑	I borrowed/was given this	❑
or mass merchandiser		book	

4. On average, how many Harlequin and Silhouette books do you buy at one time?

I buy _____ books at one time	❑
I rarely buy a book	❑

MRQ403HH-1A

5. How many times per month do you shop for any *Harlequin and/or Silhouette* books?
One answer only, please.

1 or more times a week	❏	a few times per year	❏
1 to 3 times per month	❏	less often than once a year	❏
1 to 2 times every 3 months	❏	never	❏

6. When you think of your ideal heroine, which *one* statement describes her the best?
One answer only, please.

She's a woman who is strong-willed		She's a desirable woman	❏
She's a woman who is needed by others	❏	She's a powerful woman	❏
She's a woman who is taken care of	❏	She's a passionate woman	❏
She's an adventurous woman		She's a sensitive woman	❏

7. The following statements describe types or genres of books that you may be
interested in reading. Pick *up to 2 types* of books that you are most interested in.

I like to read about truly romantic relationships	❏
I like to read stories that are sexy romances	❏
I like to read romantic comedies	❏
I like to read a romantic mystery/suspense	❏
I like to read about romantic adventures	❏
I like to read romance stories that involve family	❏
I like to read about a romance in times or places that I have never seen	❏
Other: _____	❏

*The following questions help us to group your answers with those readers who are
similar to you. Your answers will remain confidential.*

8. Please record your year of birth below.
19 _____

9. What is your marital status?

single ❏   married ❏   common-law ❏   widowed ❏
divorced/separated ❏

10. Do you have children 18 years of age or younger currently living at home?

yes ❏   no ❏

11. Which of the following best describes your employment status?

employed full-time or part-time ❏   homemaker ❏   student ❏
retired ❏   unemployed ❏

12. Do you have access to the Internet from either home or work?

yes ❏   no ❏

13. Have you ever visited eHarlequin.com?

yes ❏   no ❏

14. What state do you live in?

_____

15. Are you a member of Harlequin/Silhouette Reader Service?

yes ❏   Account # _____   no ❏   MRQ403HH-1B

If you enjoyed what you just read,
then we've got an offer you can't resist!

Take 2 bestselling love stories FREE!

Plus get a FREE surprise gift!

COMING NEXT MONTH FROM

HARLEQUIN HISTORICALS®

- **THE IMPOSTOR'S KISS**
  by **Tanya Anne Crosby,** Harlequin Historical debut
  On a quest to discover his past, the Prince of Merrick masqueraded
  as his highway-robber twin brother and found the life and the love
  he'd always dreamed of in Chloe Simon. But would Chloe forgive
  him when she learned his true identity?
  HH #683 ISBN# 29283-X $5.25 U.S./$6.25 CAN.

- **THE EARL'S PRIZE**
  by **Nicola Cornick,** author of THE NOTORIOUS MARRIAGE
  Ever since her father ruined them at the gaming tables,
  Amy Bainbridge has lived in genteel poverty and has vowed never to
  love a gambler. But when she meets Joss, the Earl of Tallant and an
  unredeemable rogue, she risks losing her heart and becoming the
  rake's prize!
  HH #684 ISBN# 29284-8 $5.25 U.S./$6.25 CAN.

- **THE SURGEON**
  by **Kate Bridges,** author of THE MIDWIFE'S SECRET
  When his troop played a prank on him, John Calloway, a mounted
  police surgeon, found himself stuck with an unwanted mail-order
  bride. Though he wanted nothing more than to send the stubborn
  beauty back home, he needed to know if she could help him find
  his long-buried heart....
  HH #685 ISBN# 29285-6 $5.25 U.S./$6.25 CAN.

- **OKLAHOMA BRIDE**
  by **Carol Finch,** author of BOUNTY HUNTER'S BRIDE
  Feisty Karissa Baxter wanted to secure land for her injured brother
  by illegally sneaking into Oklahoma Territory, but Commander
  Rafe Hunter stood directly between her and her crusade. Though
  she was breaking the law he had sworn to uphold, Rafe couldn't
  deny his smoldering passion!
  HH #686 ISBN# 29286-4 $5.25 U.S./$6.25 CAN.

KEEP AN EYE OUT FOR ALL FOUR OF THESE TERRIFIC NEW TITLES